Love Circles

Charles Lee Robinson, Jr.

Strategic Book Publishing and Rights Co.

Strategic Book Publishing and Rights Co., LLC
USA | Singapore
www.sbpra.com

For information about special discounts for bulk purchases, please contact Strategic Book Publishing and Rights Co., LLC Special Sales, at bookorder@sbpra.net.

ISBN: 978-1-68181-008-9

I would like to dedicate this book to my mother, Elaine Denise Robinson, who is no longer with us but certainly not forgotten. I would also like to dedicate this to my children, Charles Lee Robinson III (Mookie), Chacoura Robinson, and Johanna Edwards; my father, Charlie Robinson; my sisters, Celesteen Robinson, Patrice Perez, and Deanna Robinson; my brother, LaRon Robinson; my nieces and nephews; and my grandmothers, Shirley Johnson and Virginia Robinson.

These people have been very instrumental in my life, and I love them all. I thank God for blessing me with a wonderful family.

Acknowledgments

I would like to thank the following people: Oscar Beasley, Willie Hawkins, Walter Monroe, Carla Johnson, Thomas Johnson, Gerald Moxely, Ronald Myricks, Chelese Monroe, Shantella Phillips, Leola McKee, Martin Doyle, Jerrod Junious, Corey Beasley, Tynniece Phillips, Louis Lee (LuLu), Lorrie Ann Hawkins, Terry Coley, Shannon Sims, Kelvon Phillips, Darrick Turner, Lisa Finley, Phyllis Heard, Donald Charles, James Thomas Jr., Joshua Rivera Jacob Stanley, Anita Anderson, Larry Scott, Marlon Anderson, Allen Joyner, Sharon Tatum, Paulette Ranger, Reggie Jefferson, Denise Joyner, Rayjaun Tramel, Jerry Dukes, Mary Dukes, Ronald Jefferson, John Moore, William Russell, Cory Miller, Clinton Anderson, Kelwin Brown, Greg McKnight, Dave Howard, Loryn Concepcion, Marilyn Schutte, Darwin Perry, Terrance McClary, Sandra Heard, Latrice Thomas, Sarah Calhoun, William Russell, Jacqueline Heard, Jerome Brown, Carl Calhoun, Albert Calhoun, Kevin J. Johnson, Dr. Jerry G. Houston, and Nickol Lowry.

I would like to thank my family and friends for being a part of my growth and for being a very big part of my life. I wouldn't be the person I am today without all these wonderful people who have come into my life. I would like to take this time to thank you all. To those I have not mentioned, you are definitely not forgotten. I appreciate you deeply.

Contents

Introduction

This is a story about three longtime friends who are happily married. They get together for the first time in a long time and start to reminisce about all the bad relationships they've had.

They have been betrayed by their loved ones and even some family members, so they set out to get revenge. They realize that they are getting revenge on the people that hurt them, but if the people don't know that they are getting them back, then how is it revenge?

By the end they realize that the best thing to do is put revenge in God's hands. They also learn that doing the same thing over and over again yields the same results. Sometimes it's good to recognize this cycle and switch up things to bring about change.

Although *Love Circles* is a fictional story, there is a real lesson to be learned. Lenny, Richard, and Nathan go through many trials and tribulations before realizing that life can be a vicious cycle of events if they don't recognize the pattern. The three men put their hearts and lives on the line in the name of vengeance. They finally become real men and accept their losses at the end, when God blesses them with beautiful wives and wonderful families. I hope my readers enjoy this story about these three men, their true friendship that has lasted over twenty-five years, and their triumph over misdirection. This is only the beginning.

Prologue

The Guys Meet

One morning I received a call from Richard, one of my closest friends. "Hey, Lenny, what are you doing this weekend?" he asked.

"I don't have any plans yet," I replied.

"I'm thinking about calling up Nathan so that we all can get together this weekend. We've been friends for twenty-five years and we don't hang out as much as we used to do."

"Yeah, you're right," I agreed. "I'll give Nathan a call too and see what's up. We can all meet this weekend at the new jazz lounge downtown on State Street."

So I called Nathan, and he agreed that it would be a men's night out. We were all happily married, so we spent a lot of time with our families now.

My friends and I have been through hell and back with bad relationships. Finally God has sent the angels that were made for us—our wives and families. After all the madness, there was light at the end of the tunnel. I really missed my boys, though. We all were close and never crossed each other. Others had fallen by the wayside because they couldn't be trusted, but not this group of guys.

That Friday after work, we all met up at the three-story jazz house club. The club was a sight to see, and people said some rich guys owned it.

The first story was very dark with candles, dim lights, and a live jazz band that was out of this world. Of course, I arrived first. Then Richard came in after me. We shook hands and then gave each other a quick hug. We couldn't believe how fast time had flown by.

Richard and I started looking around while talking. There was a patio out back with a waterfall. Then we hit the spiral staircase on the side of the club and went up to the second story.

That's when my phone rang loudly. "Hello?" I said at the top of my lungs so the person on the other end could hear me.

"Hey, my brother, this is Nathan and I am in the building."

"Okay, where are you exactly?" I asked loudly to be heard over the music.

"I just walked in the door on the first floor, and they have a nice jazz band here," Nathan said. I could hear people in the background talking as the jazz music played. "Man, this place is nice."

I told Nathan that we were on the second floor, where they had an R&B setting. Everywhere we looked there were black leather sofas. They had three bars and a nice-sized dance floor. The DJ sat in back of one of the bars on a stage with several TVs showing videos while the music was playing.

So Nathan met us upstairs and we were all hugs and smiles. We were family, and we had come a long way since the old days. One of us was heavier and the other gray, but of course I looked the same because I stayed working out in the gym.

We went up to the bar to get our drinks, and Richard started drilling Nathan. "Boy, you don't need any drinks with that big belly you have. It looks like you drank up the whole bar already."

We started laughing loudly. Then Nathan drilled Richard back. "Boy, you need to eat. Just look at the way your two back pockets are clapping each other. You look like you have your own audience. Hey, bartender, get this man some smothered wings."

It was so funny that I was now in tears from laughing so hard. We had really missed one another. It was just like old times. I wasn't much of a driller, but I knew how to laugh. I laughed hard until tears came down my face, and that alone made us crack up. So we started ordering our drinks. I had a shot of Jack Daniels, Richard had a shot of Hennessey, and Nathan had a shot of vodka because he said he didn't like brown liquor, which he said made him sick.

We all posted up at the bar just looking around. We couldn't believe all the people who were in this place. Everyone was well dressed and looking classy. The women were gorgeous in their dresses and heels, and they all smelled really good.

Most of the guys were in jeans or slacks with button-down shirts and sports jackets, and once in a while there would be a guy dressed like an old Mack Daddy pimp. They were so funny, walking around wearing those big hats.

The second floor had chandeliers hanging everywhere. It was a much different setting from the jazz section downstairs. This place was very upscale. After we finished our drinks, we headed to the third story, where they played rap and hip-hop music. As soon as we made it to the third floor, we went to the bar and ordered more drinks.

As we took post at this large, circular bar, we bobbed our heads to 2Pac's song "How Do You Want It?" The dance floor was full. Absolutely no one was sitting down.

"Man, this place must cost a fortune," I said.

"Yes, sir, I bet it did. It's nice," Richard agreed.

"I wish I could afford a place like this," said Nathan.

"No, you just wish you could afford a *place*," Richard said to him.

I hit Richard on the arm and we started cracking up, but Nathan just stuck up his middle finger at Richard. As we went to the other side of the bar, we noticed that we were being watched.

"Do you see those women over there staring at us?" Nathan asked.

Richard joked, "Yeah, they're wondering how many months pregnant you are."

We all starting laughing. These boys always ragged on each other, but it was funny because it was all in fun. They had been this way since we were young.

"Y'all need to stop drilling on each other with y'all crazy selves," I said.

The boys wouldn't let up on each other, but that just made our meeting up so much better. We walked and talked some more. When we looked down at our glasses, we realized it was time for a refill. So back to the bar we went.

We were really starting to feel those drinks. I suggested that we go to the back of the bar, where they had a patio on the rooftop of the third story.

There were a lot of lights back there and another circular bar. They even had a pool up there. I mean, the place was so together. It had everything.

So we found a place to sit and started talking about our wives and families. I had been married to Nakia now for fifteen years, Richard had been married to Jeanette for twelve years, and Nathan had been married just five years to Shanté. We all were happy. It had been a struggle because the relationships we'd had in the past were so bad that our lives had sometimes been at stake.

As we started getting into it, the waitress came to our table and asked us if we wanted another drink. We all had that "one more drink." We were already feeling nice.

I had been in so many relationships that I never thought God would send me the right woman. I had done some things that I wasn't proud of. Nathan and Richard both agreed with that.

"I couldn't imagine my life without Nakia," I said, as I sipped slowly on my drink.

"Yeah, I know what you mean," Richard said. "Jeanette is the best."

"Shanté is that queen that every man wants," Nathan said with a smile on his face.

I took a deep breath and began telling them about all the madness that I had to go through to get where I was today. Life wasn't easy, and I just had to roll with the punches.

I could see Richard and Nathan tuning in to what I had to say. Some of my life stories they knew about, but not all. These were my boys, my family, so I began telling them about my journey.

Part One

Lenny's Story

Chapter One

Tammy, My First Love

I was seventeen when I met my first love one weekend at the skating rink. It was a Saturday evening when we first laid eyes on one another.

I was nervous at first, and then finally I got up the nerve to approach her and ask her for her name. "Excuse me. Hello, may I ask your name? I see you over here, looking so sexy."

She smiled and started to blush. "Hello, my name is Tammy."

"Hi, my name is Lenny. How are you doing tonight?"

We started talking, and then all of a sudden she grabbed my hands and started asking questions. "Do you have a girlfriend? Please be honest."

"No, I don't have anyone at the moment, so that's why I'm over here talking to you," I said with a big smile on my face. "What about yourself? Do you have a boyfriend? I bet they're lining up for you."

Then we both started smiling. Yes, we both were single and just waiting on that right person to come along. We exchanged phone numbers right before the skating rink closed. As we left the building, we started staring at each other from afar. I was just hoping that I would get that phone call from her once I got home.

The next day she called me, and from then on we would call each other every day. We really started getting into each other. We would stay on the phone all day after school and on the weekends. We would talk about almost everything and laugh at each other's crazy jokes.

Then we found out that we attended the same high school. We hadn't even realized it because we never saw each other in the halls or anything. I thought our meeting like this was fate. So one day I introduced Tammy to my best friend, George.

"George, this is Tammy. Tammy, this is my best friend, George," I said.

They stared at each other with blank looks on their faces. Tammy just nodded and started walking away very fast. I noticed that when George first saw her, he had a shocked look on his face and put his head down. I wasn't sure what it was about, but I knew I'd seen it. I folded my hands and asked him, "G, what do you think about my new girlfriend, Tammy?"

"I think she's all right. Plus, we already know each other from the past. We went to elementary school together." He paused. "And she used to be my childhood girlfriend back then."

I was stunned because Tammy had just nodded her head without saying a word. I had felt a little tension when I introduced them.

"We were only kids back then." George reassured me.

"Did you care about her, man? Do you still care about her? Come on, G, tell me something." I was asking him all kinds of questions because I had to know before I got serious with her.

"It was only puppy love."

"Okay. Are you sure, man? Because it looked like something when I introduced the two of you."

"No, Lenny, I was just shocked to see the two of you together as a couple. We liked each other when we were kids—our families are really close, so that just blew me away."

For some reason I didn't believe him. I let it go, because he was my friend and he had no reason to lie to me. So after that discussion with G, Tammy and I became closer. I went over to her house every day. We had a lot of fun together and had a lot of good conversations. Her mother and father loved me. Tammy had three brothers, and she was the second oldest child—the only girl. They were cool, and we all became good friends.

One day, while talking on the phone, we brought up sex. The conversation became tense. Both of us were virgins, and the curiosity was starting to build up inside us. We were ready to explode. We were curious and excited as we talked more about it. Then I heard the magic words come out of her mouth. She said, "I want you to be my first, Lenny."

I was flattered that she had chosen me, but everything I knew about sex was based on what I'd seen on the pornos we had stolen from G's father's room.

After that conversation we made plans to have our first time with one another. She told me that her mom and dad were going out of town that coming weekend. Her brothers were going to be at their cousin's house. I was so damn happy that I started jumping on my bed like I was a little kid.

This is perfect, I thought. I went to the store and bought some protection. I had to read the instructions because I had never used a condom.

When the weekend finally came, I was so nervous. Our hearts were pounding so damn hard, and butterflies filled my stomach. Goosebumps broke out on my arms and chest like I had a rash or something. I think I was so scared that my dark-skinned complexion turned light-skinned.

We started kissing and rubbing each other. Next thing we knew, we were really starting to get into each other. It felt so nice—at least to me. It was good, but we were so inexperienced.

From that day on we talked about sex all the time. It was addictive, like a drug. We were like a couple of horny dogs. We would have sex under the kitchen table, on the kitchen table, on the dining room floor—nothing was off-limits to us. Tammy and I promised never to let each other go.

"Lenny, I won't ever let you go," Tammy said.

"Tammy, that's the way I feel too, so let's pinky-swear on it," I said, as I was in puppy love. So we hooked pinkies, and then shared a long, passionate kiss.

Sometimes when her mom and dad were home, we would sneak downstairs and have sex in the basement. That was very scary, though, because her dad was a very big man. He was six foot three and about three hundred pounds. He was built like a defensive end on a football team.

"What if your father catches us, girl? Then what are we going to say?" I asked.

"Stop worrying so much. My dad sleeps very deeply and won't wake up," she responded. "Plus, my parents might be doing their own thing, so stop worrying." She said that all the time and was constantly telling me not to worry, so like a fool I took my chances.

Tammy and I went everywhere together, and I even took her over to George's house. George's sister, Donna, became good friends with Tammy. Sometimes I would pop up at G's house and Tammy would already be over there. I thought it was okay because Tammy and Donna had become good friends.

Then, all of a sudden, Tammy started picking fights with me—I mean, for no reason she would start arguments. I didn't know what was going on with her. She would get upset about small things but made them seem big.

So I decided that I would break up with her for a while so that she could get herself together. I told her that "I will give you a chance to get yourself together, girl, because you keep making up arguments with me for nothing." I didn't like to argue, so I thought it was best that we go our own ways, but I was only thinking temporarily. "Tammy, I think we need time away from each other." I had a serious look on my face.

"That's cool with me. Bye," she said with a nasty attitude.

"Damn, are you on your period or something?" I asked her.

"Are you on yours?" she retorted.

I was shocked that she was acting this way, so I walked off and said, "Good-bye, Tammy."

I told George about it, and all he said was, "Man, stay strong and you'll get back together."

"I guess you're right, G."

After that I wouldn't even look another girl's way because I thought of Tammy all the time. But she didn't call me anymore; everything just stopped. I stopped seeing her in school. It was like she had just disappeared.

One day I was bored, so I went to G's house, and who did I see there? Tammy. George was at the door as she was leaving, and he didn't have a shirt on.

I thought to myself, *What the hell?* Then I thought maybe she was there to see Donna.

This went on for months, and every time she saw me, she wouldn't even speak. She acted as if I had done something really bad to her.

Then rumors starting going around the school, and at first that was all I thought they were. Then one day at school people started coming up to me saying that Tammy and George were a couple. I just ignored all that nonsense. The more I heard, though, the more hurt and in disbelief I was because I just knew they wouldn't do that to me. So every time people came up to me and asked, I would yell at them and say, "Get the hell out of here with that nonsense. Where are you getting this stuff from?"

I thought that people were just trying to ruin our friendship, but more rumors kept popping up. Then one day a big rumor came out: someone said that Tammy was pregnant by George. That one really pissed me off. It shocked the hell out of me. I had to confront G about this one.

"Hey, there's a rumor saying that you got Tammy pregnant, and that you all are a couple," I said to him.

"No way, man. They're just trying to ruin our friendship 'cause they're all jealous," he said.

"My bad, G. I shouldn't have even doubted you. I'm sorry, man," I said sadly. I just couldn't understand why someone would make up something like this. It was just so crazy to me.

As the months went on, he could no longer deny it because she was starting to show. I acted like it didn't hurt me, but it burned me up inside.

From that day forward, I no longer looked at him as a brother or as a best friend. I hated the sight of his lying ass. She was no longer anything to me. All I could think about was how she had betrayed me with my best friend. I hated her guts because everybody else knew before I did.

George and I stopped talking for a long while. Somehow he managed to blame it all on her though, so we became friends again—but we weren't nearly as close as we had been in the past.

One week G and I decided to go skating together. After skating, some guys surrounded G. I pulled him out of the circle and said loudly to them all, "Nobody's jumping my friend. You will have to go through me first."

"Oh yeah? We'll see about that," one of the guys said with anger in his voice.

Before I could say something else, George took off and left me standing alone. So I ran, too.

G wasn't as fast as I was, though, because he was always very slow. They caught him and began to put in work. I ran over and got them off of him. G started running again, and then I heard Tammy screaming frantically.

"Run, G, run!" she kept saying over and over again. Even though my adrenaline was up, I could hear her from way down the street, and not once did I hear run Lenny run. If it wasn't for him, I wouldn't ever have run. That hurt me to my heart when I realized she was thinking of his safety and not mine. I had to be really strong so I ignored it, but I couldn't forget it. It played over and over in my mind.

I knew at that moment I had to get them back, especially G for making a mockery of our friendship. So I started flirting with all his old girlfriends. I knew some of Tammy's friends liked me, so I started flirting with her friends too.

I finally ran into Janice, a girl G used to see a lot at one time. He used to brag about how good she was in bed and what he used to do to her all the time. I pulled Janice aside one day and told her that I had a crush on her. She didn't believe me and thought I was joking, plus she knew how close G and I were. At one time she thought we were brothers. I think she thought I was trying to set her up or something. But I was serious, and I let it be known to her that I wanted her.

I finally convinced her that I wanted her and told her she was just going to have to trust that I wouldn't go back and tell G anything about her. It took a while, but I finally talked her into coming over to my house. My parents were out of town, so we would have a place to be alone.

"I knew you cared about G, so I stayed back," I said.

Janice said, "He probably would be mad at both of us now, Lenny."

"So what? He's got another girl, so please stop worrying about him, Janice."

So after the sweet-talking, we went in my room and had sex for about an hour and a half. The sex was good, just as G had told me. I felt much better, because I felt I had accomplished something. I had finally gotten back at G. The only problem was, he never knew about it, so revenge didn't feel as good as I thought it would.

Yes, yes. I got him back. Now it's her turn, I thought. I started flirting with Tammy's girlfriends. Dana used to stare at me all the time, even when I used to be with Tammy, so I chose to go after her. That would be the last one Tammy would ever expect, I thought. She would be perfect to get Tammy back. I was on a mission to hurt her heart just as she had done to mine, and I really didn't care anymore.

So one day Dana and I exchanged numbers. We began talking on the phone and flirting all the time. We would fondle each other in the hallways at school. I finally talked her into coming over to my uncle's house.

We had sex all over my uncle's house, and it was way better than what Tammy had to offer. She was way more advanced than Tammy. That was the first time a girl gave me oral sex. I tell you, my toes wouldn't stop curling up.

Revenge felt so sweet. I had gotten both of them back. They thought that they were getting away with what they had done to me. In the end I felt I had the last laugh. Life was so funny, and karma was a mutha. But, again, I only felt good for a moment.

How am I going to make it known to Tammy? Did I really get them back? I asked myself.

Chapter Two

When I Met Macey

After I got Tammy and George behind me, I graduated from high school. I chose not to go to college, so I got myself a nice job that paid a fairly decent wage. One day at work I met a girl named Macey.

She would come to my job all the time with her mother, so I started flirting with her. Then one day I started talking to her, and we wound up exchanging phone numbers. She was short in stature but very curvy, with a beautiful smile, long real hair, and a pretty chocolate skin tone.

We began talking, and I started going over to her house. Sometimes I would pick her up and bring her to my house. I met her mother, who was really down to earth, and she immediately liked me. She just loved me to death. Macey also had an aunt who lived with them. Her name was Dina, and she loved me too. So I became a part of her family, and they treated me well.

Macey and I talked, and she told me that she was still a virgin. I was actually surprised. She let me know that she wasn't sure if she was ready to give it up yet. I thought every young girl at her age had already lost her virginity, but I guess I was wrong.

I let her know that I would be patient and that I respected her no matter what, so I continued to see her. I really liked her for her and not because of what she had between her legs. At least that's how I felt at first, but after a while of not having sex, things started to get frustrating. We weren't having sex, but we sure were talking about it a whole lot.

I asked her, "Girl, are you ready yet? You're going to make a brother catch blue balls or something."

"I don't know yet, Lenny. Baby, I need more time, okay?" she said. Even though she wasn't ready, I knew that I was.

I stayed faithful to her and never cheated on her or anything, but boy was I horny. Even though I was getting that urge, I really just wanted to wait on her until she was ready. I went months without having sex because I really cared about her—but, *man*, it was killing me.

We would walk in the park and talk about our future together, and it felt so good to know that she wanted to be a part of mine. We would even talk about having children one day.

It felt so good to be with her even though we had never had any sexual contact. I just enjoyed her.

As time went on Macey became a little more curious about sex for some reason, and she would ask me questions while acting shy.

"How does sex feel, Lenny?" she asked.

"It feels good. It's a feeling that you can't explain with words."

"My cousins say that sex hurts at first. Is that true?"

"Don't listen to them. Everybody is different and every experience is different," I said.

Then we started rubbing and kissing, and my heart would flutter when I was with her. We would go to the mall all the time, and I loved spending money on her. I would buy her new outfits, and I kept her in the latest fashions. I showed her how a woman was supposed to be treated. I spoiled her and treated her like a queen every time I got the chance because that is what a man is supposed to do for his woman. Sometimes we would exchange gifts with each other.

After shopping in the mall one day, Macey said, "I want to be with you and only you, Lenny."

"I feel the same way about you, Little Miss Chocolate," I laughed.

She loved it when I called her "Chocolate"; her eyes would light up and a big smile would appear on her face. She had me feeling her so much that I wouldn't even look at another girl because she made me feel complete.

I remember one day while driving around, Macey saw this girl she didn't like. She pointed her out and started talking about the girl as if she were a dog. She wouldn't tell me what the feud was about, so I didn't ask. We just rode on by and I left it alone.

As the days went by, I was getting a little more impatient with Macey because I was used to having sex and now my sex life was nonexistent. It felt like it was killing me. My flesh was definitely getting the best of me. I explained to Macey what was going on with me because I felt communication was the best thing to have in a relationship. "I promise, when the time comes you will be my first," she said.

"I hope so, because I keep having wet dreams all over the place," I replied.

Macey started laughing, and then she shook her head up and down as if I was crazy.

One day Macey's cousin threw a really nice party. Everyone was having a good time dancing all over the place. Macey did not want to leave my side, so she stayed stuck to me like glue. Even if I had wanted to shake her, I couldn't. I thought it was cute, though.

She whispered in my ear softly, "My cousins are sneaky and I don't trust them, so I am not leaving you around for them to eat you up." I looked at her and started laughing with my hand over my mouth. "For real, they might try and talk to you." She looked so serious.

I just smirked and said, clear as day, "Nah, I don't think so."

"Yeah, I do think so, because they are trifling."

As the night went on, everybody was getting drunk. Most of her cousins were female. Even though she did have some very nice-looking cousins, I still wouldn't have left her for them because my heart was with her.

I saw that some of her cousins were on the dance floor showing off and dancing really nasty. I saw out of the corner of my eye that they were staring at me on the sly. One of them was even looking at me like I was eye candy or something.

Some of them were even trying to pull on me on the sly, but I didn't tell Macey because she would blow a damn gasket. So the party ended on a very good note.

The day after the party, Macey told me that she was ready to make love to me. I almost choked on the food I was eating. I was so shocked when she told me that, I couldn't do anything but stutter. "Wh-wh-wh-what did you say? Huh? What?"

"That's right—you heard me. Oh, what, are you scared now?" she asked. "I'm really feeling the connection with you, and I trust you."

"Are you sure that you're ready?" I asked. "Girl, I hope you're not playing with me."

"Boy, I'm sure, I'm sure, I'm sure," she repeated over and over.

So we made plans to try to be alone at her mother's house when no one was home. It was a Friday, and I remember it well because her mother went out of town that weekend. She left Macey home alone, but her aunt Dina still had access to the house, so we had to be careful. Dina was supposed to be gambling that weekend at a card game. She loved playing cards. The card game was on the other side of town, so we lay on the couch and began kissing and touching each other's bodies.

Her body was flawless and fresh and pure because it had never been touched. She had the curves of a goddess. Her breasts were not too small and not too big; they were perfect, and I mean *perfect*. She was so sexy and pretty that lying next to her gave me butterflies. She was all that and more.

She let her hair down. It was long and black and very shiny, and it smelled great. Her eyes went in the back of her head as I kissed her all over. She was mesmerized. She had never felt this way before because no man had ever touched her. I was the first ever.

As I began to take off her bra strap, she became more tense and afraid. I whispered in her ear, softly saying, "Trust me. Please just let go and trust me."

I could tell that the tense feeling was still there because her body was still stiff. I got all the way down to her belly button with my lips, kissing her gently. Then I tried to pull her panties down slowly. At first she held on to them for about ten seconds. Then she looked down at me and said, "Please don't hurt me."

"I promise I won't hurt you," I said.

Then she finally released her panties as she inhaled slowly. At that point I could tell that she trusted me, so I pulled them down. Then I grabbed my protection and put it on. I began to rub my tubesteak on her cookie, and I could feel it getting so wet.

Several times I tried to penetrate her but could not. I stayed calm and continued to let her know that she was in good hands. "Baby, stay still. I got you," I said a few times in her ear, and I could see on her skin that my voice gave her chills. She began squirming and moaning, but still wasn't sure.

Her body became so tense, and she began moving away. I finally got her to relax for a moment and got the tip of my penis in. As soon as I was about to thrust—

Boom, boom, boom.

It was a knock at the door, and we both jumped wildly. We put on our clothes so fast. When we got to the door, we saw that it was Macey's aunt Dina. She had lost all her money at the card game already, and now she wanted to crash our party.

"Why are you back, Auntie?" Macey asked. "Are you broke already?"

"Yeah, they got me that fast," Aunt Dina said. She turned to Macey with a smile on her face and asked, "Why? What are y'all doing, trying to have sex?"

"No, we weren't, so stop saying that, Aunt Dina."

"Would I do that?" I asked with a smirk on my face.

She started laughing, and so did Macey and I. Aunt Dina was so damn tipsy, but she was always down to earth. She went staggering into the bedroom off the kitchen. I heard her as she plopped herself on the bed, and the next thing I heard was her snoring loudly.

Macey and I looked at each other. I said, "Wow, that was close—and I mean that was too close for comfort."

"You are definitely right about that, Lenny. Her drunk behind almost caught us," she said. We smiled at each other as the sweat rolled down our foreheads. Then I went home.

Macey and I tried to have sex a few more times, but we always got interrupted or she was just too scared.

One day we were talking on the phone and Macey said, "I'm going to hang with my cousins today." I guess they were having girls' night out or something.

"Okay, Macey, go ahead and enjoy your family," I said.

So I hung out for a few hours by myself, and it gave me time to think. After driving around for a while, I found myself missing her more and more. Something told me to drive by her house, and as soon as I turned that corner, I saw Macey standing in front of her house.

All her female cousins were there, and so were a bunch of guys I didn't know. I could see this young guy all up in Macey's face, and she was just giggling and talking to him. I guess he was spitting some good game to her, because even though she was dark-skinned, you could see her blushing all over the place.

I was so jealous and very upset with her, and I didn't know what to do because I was totally in shock. This had really caught me off guard. My hands began to shake and I started sweating profusely. I shut my eyes and hoped that this was a very bad dream. When I opened my eyes, reality really hit me hard. *Why would she do this to me?* I asked myself.

As I pulled up, I could see the shocked look on Macey's face. It was priceless.

"What are you doing out here, Macey?" I asked in a deep, manly tone.

"I'm not doing anything. We're all are just having a good time," she said. "Why are you asking me that question?" She asked this loudly, as if to embarrass me.

"So who are these guys? I thought you were only hanging out with your cousins?" I asked.

"These are some of my friends from school, and some are from the neighborhood. Why are you asking me all these questions? What? I can't have any male friends?"

"I didn't say that, but this guy was all up in your face, like y'all are dating or something. I've never seen him before, and you definitely never introduced us."

"I don't care if you've ever seen them or not," she said to me with an attitude.

"Go in the house, Macey," I said. I couldn't think of anything else to say to her.

"No, I don't have to," she said very loudly.

Then the guy that she was talking to got very nasty with me and said, "Man, she doesn't have to go nowhere."

Macey smiled when he said that, but I just ignored him because he was with his friends. I kept talking to her, but she was acting so cold. This guy kept saying smart stuff to me because he had all his backup with him. I just looked at him, turned my head, and kept trying to convince her that she was doing me wrong.

No matter what, Macey wasn't budging, and I was starting to look like a big fool. I looked at her one more time and said loudly, "Go in the house, Macey."

"No, I won't go in the house. You're not my father."

So I went to my car and started it up. My heart was so crushed and full of pain as I left. I never called her again.

I couldn't figure out why she had acted that way toward me. I hadn't done anything wrong to make her to treat me like that, so I was puzzled.

After that day, whenever she called me, I would just hang up the phone. I was done with her.

The phone rang again, and I would say to myself, "Here we go again." I felt she had to pay for humiliating me like that.

Then I remembered the girl she had talked about like a dog that one day. It came to me like a lightbulb turning on. I planned to talk to the girl and get Macey back for what she had done to me.

Yes, revenge was on my mind .I didn't care anymore. She would pay for doing me that way.

One day I saw the girl Macey hated most. I picked her up and asked, "Would you like to go on a stroll?"

Of course, she said yes. Her name was Penny, and she was the cutest little thing. She was very short, with pretty big brown eyes, light brown complexion, and a nice ass on her. We rode around for a while, and I made it my business to ride down Macey's street. Macey was so pissed when she saw Penny and me riding down her street. I could see the anger on her face as we cruised on by. Macey called that night, and I just hung up on her ass.

Chapter Three

Penny

Penny didn't like Macey either, and I didn't understand what in the world their beef was about. For some reason they couldn't explain why they hated each other so much, and that drove me crazy. Macey called Penny a whore and Penny called Macey a bitch, and judging by the way she said it, I could tell she meant it. I didn't understand the hatred they had for each other. "That bitch thinks she is the shit," Penny said.

Anyway, apart from her differences with my ex, I thought that Penny was a very nice girl. I knew that I was only talking to Penny out of revenge against Macey, so there wasn't any real connection between us. I started seeing that Penny was really starting to have strong feelings for me. She started offering to take me out to dinner. We went walking on the pier at the beach, and the walks were really nice. One day while we were walking and holding hands, Penny turned to me and asked, "What did you see in that bitch Macey?"

It caught me off guard, and I shrugged my shoulders and said, "I really don't know. Let's talk about something else." To change the subject, I asked, "Penny, why were you single? I know you could get a man if you wanted one." I was hoping that this would steer the conversation away from Macey, and it worked like a charm.

"I broke up with this guy named KC because he didn't spend any time with me," she said. "I think he was a big player or something.

Why else wouldn't he want to spend time with me?" I could tell that she really cared about him by the way she looked and the way she answered my questions. Then I thought to myself for a second and said, "KC. I know a guy who goes by that name. If it's the same one, he's a friend of mine. Is his last name Couch?" I hoped it wasn't the same KC. I could tell by the look on her face that she was hoping it wasn't the same guy either.

"Why, do you know him?" she asked with a very disappointed look on her face.

"Yes, I do know him. Actually, I was talking to him a few days ago," I said. KC and I had been hanging out for a while now.

"It wasn't serious, Lenny. I promise you, it really wasn't," Penny said. Then I gave her that look as if to say, *Are you for real?* I guess she didn't really know what to say to me, because she just kept trying to explain herself. She saw my reaction when I realized that we were talking about the same guy and kept trying to get me to believe that they weren't really dealing with each other on a serious level. I wasn't trying to judge her or anything, but I just didn't want any problems with my friend. Plus, I was thinking about what had happened with George and Tammy. That situation stayed in my mind, and I didn't want to repeat that crazy mess ever again. So I was hesitant this time around. I wanted to know everything. I was making certain that I wouldn't be in the dark about things this time around. There was no way I was going through that again.

"Penny, did you and KC sleep together? Please tell me, because I really need to know," I said. "Please tell me no."

She put her head down for a second. Then she looked up at me and said, "We tried to have sex, but nothing happened."

"What you mean you tried and nothing really happened? You have to explain that one to me." I was so upset that I was at a loss for words for a second. "I will talk to you later. I really can't talk right now."

I saw the tears running down Penny's face as I left. For some reason I had to be alone after hearing all that bad news. I told my friend Johnny about the situation, and he said, "Man, you better go ahead and get some of that because KC won't find out." Then he paused for a second and said, "He didn't care about her anyway, or else why would he have let her go?"

"Are you sure?" I sighed "I don't know if it's right to talk to her, Johnny, especially if KC had her. You know how cool we are."

"Believe me, man, he doesn't have feelings for her," he said with a laugh. It wasn't funny to me, though. I felt deep down in my bones that it was the wrong thing to do. "He told me that he was only with her because he wanted to break her virginity and be her first."

I couldn't believe what I was hearing. I thought KC had way more class than that, but I guess not. Johnny looked so serious as he was telling me all this bad stuff about KC. Then I thought to myself, *Is that damn KC really a dog like that?* That just didn't sound like the same guy I had been hanging with. Then my mind started to wander as I thought about what Penny had said—that they'd tried to have sex. That stayed in my mind for a while. I guess you could say that a lightbulb in my head lit up.

I said to myself, "Penny is still a virgin because she said they *tried*. She said that he never penetrated her." That made me feel a little better. "Wow, another virgin. I got myself another virgin," I said to Johnny. I told him not to tell KC that I was talking to Penny, because I felt he didn't need to know yet. Johnny promised me that he wouldn't tell KC.

Then one day I saw KC. He ran up to me and said, "I heard that you are talking to Penny, my ex." I thought he would be upset, but then a huge smile came on his face.

I was shocked. "Who told you I was talking to her?' I asked him.

"A little bird told me," he joked.

I didn't find it funny at all. I had just had that talk with Johnny. I hoped he wasn't trying to start any trouble. *These days you can't trust anybody, not even your own family*, I thought. "Do you still have feelings for her, man?" I asked him. I really needed to know before I took my relationship with Penny any further.

KC was a calm and cool type of guy, and very confident. I could tell he really didn't care about Penny; I could see it all over his face. She was just another notch in his belt. It was sad in a way, because I really believed she cared about him. Yes, he was only out for sex, but she really had her heart involved. She had no idea that she had been played. I wasn't about to tell her either; I just wanted to protect myself and get as much information out of him as I possibly could. He was a grimy dude, but I saw that he liked to brag and talk shit about Penny. He was a heartless man, and I had thought better of him.

After spilling his guts to me, he finally answered the question I had asked him earlier. "Hell no, I don't want her or care about her. You can have that, man," he said. "I don't want her ass at all." He was very cold toward her. Then he gave me a high five, got in his car, and drove off. I wondered what the hell that was all about.

I never told Penny that I had seen or talked to KC, because I was taught never to volunteer information. So I kept quiet about it. It was now six months into our relationship, and all of a sudden we started talking about sex. After planning and planning, I got the keys to my uncle's house and asked Penny, "Will you come over my uncle's house today? He gave me the keys and we will be alone."

"Yes, I would love to come over. Are you coming to get me?" Penny asked.

"Yes, I will be there to get you shortly," I said. I cleaned up my uncle's house and had it looking nice. I couldn't wait until Penny was finally here. When I picked her up and brought her back there, I already had the music playing and incense burning. I knew it would surprise her and make her feel more comfortable. I could see on her face that she was very pleased. I had the curtains closed to make it a very cozy, romantic spot. I loved the element of surprise.

I took my time relaxing her, showing her my affectionate side, and letting out all my emotions. We started kissing and breathing heavily. We really got into one another. Then, before we knew it, we were lying in bed naked, talking and just enjoying the soft music. It was very romantic, and the mood was set just right. I wanted her to feel so special, especially after hearing how KC had treated her. She deserved to be treated well.

I stroked her whole body with a soft white feather as I kissed every spot. She kept telling me that she had never felt like this before. I made her feel so special, and I whispered to her, "You're special to me, baby." Then I took the protection out of my pants pocket and put it on. I asked her softly, "Are you ready, baby?"

"Yes, yes, I'm ready, Lenny," Penny said. I had to keep trying to penetrate because she was so tense and so tight. I could see why KC hadn't been able to penetrate; her vagina was tighter than spandex, I tell you. I began to try everything to make her relax. I began doing a little foreplay on her and hoped that would do the trick. She was jumping and moving all over the place. I started to get a little frustrated because I couldn't seem to get things to work out. I think she could tell that I wasn't happy. "We can do this some other time, Penny," I said.

"Are you mad at me, Lenny?" she asked.

"No, not at all," I said.

"Why don't you keep trying?"

"This is a workout, girl,"

"I'm so sorry," she said.

"Don't be. I promise, we will try again," I told her. So we got dressed, and then I drove her home. After she got out of the car, we kissed, and then I watched her go into the house. I headed home with a lot on my mind but knew that we had to try again after getting that far.

The next time Penny came over to my uncle's, we got it on. It still took a while at first, but once we got through the first stage, it was on from there. Even though we started having sex all the time, there was something missing in our relationship. She was a little boring and not as much fun as Macey. We just didn't have that chemistry. So I started hanging out with my friends and my cousins more just to fill in that empty void. Penny would constantly ask me stupid questions and I just couldn't understand where she was coming from. "Are you still seeing Macey or something?" she would ask. "You'd better not be."

"Stop nagging me about being with Macey, girl. Are *you* seeing Macey?" I asked her, trying to be funny. "I don't want Macey. Besides, if I wanted her, then that's who I would be with."

We started spending less and less time together because I couldn't take being interrogated like that. I couldn't understand why she was always questioning me. It was becoming very annoying. Sometimes I thought she was my drill sergeant or something. I mean, she stayed on my ass like white on rice. I started asking myself, *What's revenge?* Suddenly I didn't feel so good anymore. I tried to figure out how to get out of this mess with Penny. Things had gotten worse as time went on.

Penny tried everything to make things work between us. She started buying me clothes and sneakers—anything to try to win my love. I had just lost the little bond that we'd shared. She even tried to seduce me several times, but that didn't work either, although I did fall for it a few times.

Then one day she started going down on me. I was stunned. "What are you doing down there, girl?" I asked.

"I want to perform oral sex on you," she replied.

"Where did you learn that from?" I asked her.

"I watched my brother's porno movies with my girlfriends one night," she said. "We were talking about trying it."

"Okay, we can try it," I said with the biggest smile on my face. I was in heaven. It was so good that my toes curled up and everything. I had always heard that if a woman gave you oral sex and your toes curled up, then that was a good thing. It was something new to me that just took sex to another level. I couldn't explain it in words, but at that moment I knew somehow that she was trying to hook me and keep me from leaving her. And guess what? It worked. This was something new to me, so I had to keep her around a little longer.

"Damn," I said to myself. I knew that I had to be strong to withstand this seduction. My flesh was weak.

As Penny's feelings began to grow, she began searching through my belongings while I was sleeping. Then I would catch her hiding behind buildings, watching me and making sure that I wasn't seeing Macey. She would follow me while I was driving my car. I couldn't get rid of her no matter how hard I tried. She had become a stalker and I couldn't shake her. She embarrassed me by confessing her love for me in public. "I love you and I'm never going to let you go," she said.

"You better calm your ass down, because there's a thin line between love and hate and this shit isn't cool," I said. She made me feel on edge all the time. It got to the point where I wouldn't even take her to my family functions. I just didn't want to be seen with her anymore.

"Why don't you ever take me anywhere, Lenny?" she would ask. "You're always with your friends."

"My friends know how to act and you don't," I told her. Now I could see why KC had acted so cold to her. She could provoke a man to act that way. "If you act civilized, I'll introduce you to my family."

She started tripping when I said that, so I said, "That's why I'm not taking you anywhere." I knew my mother probably wouldn't like her, so I decided to keep them far apart. She wasn't take-home-to-Mom to material. I didn't like the way she acted and I didn't want her to embarrass me. All I could think about was how to get rid of this crazy girl. By this point I wished I had never tried to get revenge on Macey. I had dug myself into an even deeper hole.

She became so damn annoying that whenever she called, I would let the phone just keep ringing. Sexual relations were dying. I got to the point where I didn't even want her to touch me. I didn't want to do foreplay anymore; I just wasn't feeling her like that. I would get straight to the point without even kissing. Once I was done, I would just get up.

One day she caught me at home while I was just relaxing and said, "Man, what the hell is wrong with you? Why you don't answer my calls anymore? Is there someone else? Tell me now."

"No, I don't answer because I don't. Plus, you give me headaches with all your questions."

She started cursing on the phone, which really turned me off. I couldn't take it anymore. "Penny I don't think we should take this relationship any further," I said.

"I don't care what you say because you are mine forever," she said.

At that moment I knew this chick was out of her mind, maybe even a little bipolar. "You better get your obsessive ass out my life. Get it through your thick skull—it's over!" I yelled.

"No, it's not! No, it's not!" she said. She kept saying it over and over. She was sounding really crazy, and that worried me a bit. Then she started crying and boohooing all over the place, but I was not going to fall for her shit again. My plan was to get her out of my life. I told her I was going to hang up the phone, because I didn't want to hear it.

"I'm sorry! I'm sorry!" she said.

"It's too late, Penny," I said. "You made your own bed and now you have to lay in it."

"Fuck you!" she hollered.

That really tripped me out, hearing her say that. First she had apologized and now she was cursing me out. All I could do was wonder what had happened to the love. This girl had really turned out to be a nightmare. I thought revenge was supposed to make a person feel better, but I felt like shit. This would change my whole outlook on relationships.

Even though Macey had played me, I felt like meeting Penny had been even worse. It was the worst thing that I had ever done so far. I knew I had to regroup and turn over a new leaf.

Chapter Four

Meeting Meka

One day, in the summertime, I ran into my friend Jarvis. Jarvis and I had known each other for nine years. We had met playing football in our neighborhood.

He said, "I heard you've been talking to Penny."

"Not anymore. I'm single now. That girl is a little deranged, man," I said with a nervous look on my face.

"Yeah, I know. She's very dangerous," Jarvis laughed cheerfully. "Check this out, man—I've got a fine-ass cousin and she's having a barbecue at the beach with some sexy lil' friends. I want you to come."

I looked Jarvis up and down with a smirk and said, "Hell yeah, I will be there."

So we went and picked up a couple of friends—first Paul Trenton and then Landon Brown on the other side of town. Landon was cool, but he was a bit of a pretty boy, and he had the nerve to tell me that's he a player. He also told us that he bathes in women's bubble bath. He was the type of guy who didn't like to sweat often; I mean, he would show up with baby powder on his neck. We would just laugh.

As Landon got in the car, Jarvis and I looked at the pretty boy and started making faces and cracking up. Landon said, "Damn, let me in on the joke." I just nodded and said, "Nothing, man, just an inside joke." He raised his eyebrows and smirked.

Paul was the quiet type, but a very sneaky individual. You couldn't turn your back on him for a second. He would always try to make people feel sorry for him by saying his mother didn't like him, and that she had picked his younger brother as her favorite child. He never said why his mom used to feel that way, so we never assumed. We did hear that he used to steal out of her purse and always manipulated her. If you let him tell his side of the story though, it didn't really happen that way. He said he would never steal from his mother.

So we were all in the car headed to the beach, joking around and having fun. When we arrived at the beach, it was packed with kids and beautiful women. It was wonderful. The sun was at its peak, and we could see heat waves from afar. It was hot out. It was excellent beach weather, and it seemed as if the whole city was there.

I was looking for the women, who were alone together, when Jarvis pointed them out. He yelled loudly, "There they go, Lenny!"

As we walked up slowly, Jarvis introduced us. "Meka, this is Lenny."

I was like, *Damn, she's fine*, but only in my mind. Meka was so sexy and beautiful. She was light-skinned and well proportioned, kind of skinny but with a Coke-bottle figure and pretty long brown hair. She was a very pretty young woman, and when I first saw her, I was thrown off guard—almost in a state of shock. The woman was just that beautiful. As we got closer, we smelled the barbecue, so Jarvis, who loved to eat, decided to take over the girls' barbecue. That was a good thing; he was really talented at barbecuing ribs, steak, and chicken. He was a true chef.

While the ribs were cooking, Landon and I fought for Meka's attention. We were going at it. I could hardly focus because the barbecue sauce cooking on the beef ribs wafted around—believe me, everyone smelled that aroma. I couldn't wait to taste them. Meka seemed to like Landon just a little more than she liked me, so I stepped back a bit because I felt a little jealous. They were talking and laughing. It felt like I was a third wheel. They really seemed to enjoy each other's company.

I stepped back for a while and watched the two of them. Then I turned my head for one minute and Landon was gone. This was my perfect opportunity to make a move on Meka, so I ran and sat beside her with a huge smile on my face. I stared into her eyes and said to her softly, "Ol' pretty boy gone, huh?"

Meka laughed. "Ha ha. He's in the bathroom."

I wasn't trying to hate on Landon or anything, but that Meka was fine and I really wanted her. I just couldn't resist trying to steal her before he got back from the bathroom. *Plus he is taking too long in there, like he has to take a shit or something*, I thought.

I sparked up some good conversation and had Meka so intrigued that she kept smiling. By the time Landon came back, Meka was like silly putty in my hands. I could see the pain on his face. I saw him say something nasty in Jarvis's ear. I could tell that he was really pissed off and saying shit about me.

"What the hell is Lenny doing, Jarvis?" Landon whispered.

Jarvis replied quietly, "He's doing his thing, playboy. You snooze, you lose. What took you so long to come from the bathroom? Were you taking a shit?"

"Hell no," he said. Landon then gave me a nasty look. It didn't matter, though, because Meka was all mine. Just like that, I had all her attention. She started asking me all these personal questions about my life. I was like an open book and told her everything just to draw her in.

"Why have I never seen you around before? I've never seen you with my cousin," she said, without giving me a chance to even answer the first question.

I said, "I don't know why we haven't seen each other around, but maybe we did see each other and just didn't pay attention to each other like that." I paused. Then I smirked and said confidently, "It doesn't matter, though, because you see me now. And don't you like what you see?"

Meka blushed and started smiling. Her cheeks turned rose-red, as I kept laying it on thick. No matter what, Meka was going to be leaving with me and only me. The conversation was very good; there wasn't a second of silence.

"I like you, Lenny," Meka said gently but with a passionate stare. I knew at that moment, I was in good. In my mind I knew it wouldn't be long before she was my woman. We walked in the sand and then started holding hands. The sand was so warm and soothing between our toes, so we walked very slowly. As we held hands, I could feel both of our hands getting very sweaty. I guess we were both excited about the chemistry between us.

I could see Landon's face, and it looked as if he was burning up inside, like someone had poured gasoline down his throat and lit a match in his mouth. I turned my head and nodded as if to say, *Oh well.* The way I saw it, you win some and you lose some. I returned my full attention to Meka.

"I want us to get to know each really well, Lenny. I really do enjoy our conversation, and I think you are so cool," Meka said with a sexy smile.

"I feel the same way, Meka. Maybe we can take this further," I said.

"I hope so."

"I bet someone with your fine ass is already in a relationship with someone."

"No. I'm single, Lenny, but only until you ask me to be your woman," she said, smiling and blushing.

So after that day, Meka and I kept in touch. Eventually we became boyfriend and girlfriend, and we enjoyed each other. I loved being around her. It just felt so right.

Meka lived with her father and three sisters. They all were very close. I got along really well with her father and her sisters. They just loved me. Her father was a really laid-back, old-school kind of guy. He was very down to earth. He loved me as his son-in-law.

Well, her sisters didn't pull any punches; straight up, they were real chicks. One day when I was going to the bathroom, I heard Meka's sisters talking to her in the bedroom. One of them said, "What about your other boyfriend?"

I stood back in the hallway, listening to their conversation with a hurt look on my face. They thought I was still in the other room talking to their dad. I wasn't sure if the sister was asking Meka or another sister that question. I could've sworn it was directed at Meka, though. I thought to myself, *Why would they she ask her that? What are they talking about? What other boyfriend?* She had told me she was single, and I knew there wasn't anyone else because we were always on the phone and we spent so much time together. *She's got to be wrong*, I thought. I really had believed her when she told me she was single, but now I felt I was being played like a damn fool.

When Meka finally came out of the room, I pulled her aside and said, "What was your sister talking about when she mentioned your other boyfriend?"

The shock on her face told it all; she hadn't considered that I might overhear them talking. Sweat started popping off her forehead profusely. Then she spoke very nervously. "It's true, I do have somebody else, but he's in the Marines right now overseas."

"Why didn't you just tell me that from the beginning?" I asked. I was really pissed off.

"I haven't seen him in years because he's been stationed overseas, but we still keep in contact with each other, that's all," she answered calmly, with tears in her eyes. After she told me that, tears started running down my face, too. I was so hurt after hearing this news. I couldn't believe she hadn't told me.

"You know that's not right, Meka. You could've at least told me," I said.

"I know I should have told you, Lenny, but I plan on breaking up with him when he comes home," she said with little emotion.

"When is this guy supposed to return home?" I asked loudly and anxiously.

"Next weekend, so I'll break up with him then."

The week blew by so fast that it made my head spin. I was on edge. It was time for Meka's boyfriend to return home. I was so anxious because I knew she was going to make our relationship official. But when her boyfriend got back, I didn't receive a call. All of a sudden it was like I didn't exist anymore. Every time I went to her house, her family told me I had missed her by seconds.

I was so upset. How could someone who claimed she cared about me hurt me so badly? I was going through all the heartache and pain I had gone through in the past all over again. I just couldn't believe it.

Then one day I rode by McDonald's and saw Meka and her Marine boyfriend all hugged up. I could see them through the window looking all lovey-dovey. He had this huge bouquet of flowers and balloons in his hand. I watched him bend down on one knee as if he was proposing to her. Sure enough, that was exactly what he was doing.

I couldn't believe my eyes. Meka was all smiles. I was pissed off and beside myself at that moment. I put my car in gear and sped off so fast that my tires spun and left their mark on the pavement.

The next day I finally caught up with her on the telephone. She made so many excuses as to why we haven't seen each other for a week. I asked sarcastically, "Anything special happen since I last saw you a week ago?"

She said, "Brian is his name. He proposed to me, and I'm not sure whether I will accept or not."

At that moment I didn't know what to say. All I know is my heart just dropped to the floor. From that day on I was no longer the happy-go-lucky guy I had been.

Four weeks later, Meka told me that she was pregnant and that the baby was mine. I thought, *Is this a joke?* If so, it wasn't that damn funny. I looked at her in disgust and said loudly, "Hell no it isn't, so stop lying to me right now."

Meka kept trying to convince me. "The baby is yours, Lenny, I swear."

I laughed loudly in her face and said, "Not." We went on and on about it. I didn't believe her at all.

Then, to top it all off, her boyfriend, Brian, approached me with some of his friends. He said loudly, trying to embarrass me, "I heard you said the baby Meka is carrying is yours and not mine."

Brian was a very big, muscular guy, but I didn't back down when he approached me. "Do I know you, man?" I asked nervously.

"No, you don't," he said in a very deep, menacing voice.

"All right, then why would I say that?"

He was very arrogant because he was with a group of friends. I just let it go and turned my head while he was still talking. I was so pissed at him for approaching me like that. After that episode I just left Meka alone. I wouldn't answer the phone or anything. She knew where I hung out, though, so she eventually found me. I laughed in her face.

She started showing up at my cousin's house in Brian's car. I talked her into having sex in the back of Brian's car. We had his car rocking. I knew this was wrong, but I had to get him back for trying to embarrass me in front of his friends that day. At that moment I felt as if I had truly gotten his ass back.

Chapter Five

Lisa

After the breakup, Meka and I still kept in touch with each other. Sometimes she would say it was Brian's baby. She just couldn't make up her mind as to who the father really was, which made me more skeptical. She got so upset that I rejected her that she said she was moving to Alabama, where her mom had moved about two years ago. She probably wanted to be with her mom when she had her baby. She was now four months into her pregnancy. Her stomach looked just like a little bouncing ball.

The day she left for Alabama, I was so damn happy. It felt like a weight had been lifted off my shoulders. I started singing to myself loudly, "Ding dong, the bitch is gone, the bitch is gone, the little bitch is gone." That was so funny to me.

From that day on I vowed to stay single, and that's what I did. It felt so good not having that little liar Meka around. I'd thought she was the one for me, but she wasn't. It was truly over.

After that, I partied all the time. I got drunk and partied some more, and no one could stop me. One night I went out to the club and met a girl named Lisa. She was out with a few of her friends and a few cousins too. She invited me to go out to breakfast after the club. "My girls and I are going to get something to eat after the club. Do you want to go?" she asked softly in my right ear.

"What are you trying to say, that I need to eat? Why, does it look that way?" I teased.

"No, not at all. Why are you acting like that?" Lisa asked with a look of confusion.

"I thought you were saying that I need some meat on my bones," I said with my eyebrow lifted slightly.

"No, you are perfect," she said flirtatiously.

"I'm just playing with you. Sure, I'll go," I said with excitement in my voice.

"You're crazy, man. You had me thinking I said something wrong," Lisa said.

"Oh, don't mind me—I like to play sometimes," I said. We turned to each other and started laughing. We loved flirting with one another; it was exciting.

Breakfast was nice, and we had a good time as we fed our faces. I told her I didn't have a girlfriend at the moment because I had gone through a very bad breakup with my ex.

She acted like she understood what I was saying. "Are you sure? I take care of my man."

"Oh, really?" I said.

She started blowing kissing at me and smiling. I started blushing. She was really laying it on thick. I knew she had other intentions for me because I could see it in her body language, and her eyes told it all.

I knew that I wasn't going to budge. I didn't want to get into another relationship because I had been hurt so badly in the past. I was single and wanted to stay that way no matter how thick she was laying it on. I didn't care what she said. I told Lisa I wanted to stay friends and didn't want to rush into anything. Truthfully, a relationship wasn't in my near future. Lisa wasn't hearing that, though; she just let what I was saying go in one ear and out the other. I didn't want to hurt her, so I kept it real and said, "Lisa, I can't promise you anything serious right now."

As time went on, I felt like Lisa kept pushing the envelope

between us. She would call me all the time. The phone rang so damn much that I knew it was her every time. She would get upset if I didn't call her every day or answer the phone when she called.

She also started stalking me like some crazy nut. When I would wake up and get the newspaper in the morning, she would be waiting there in her car. I started thinking she was loony and joked with myself that she needed mental help. She and her cousins would ride in my neighborhood, asking my neighbors questions about me like they were damn detectives or something. At night I would glance out the window and see her riding by and slowing down to look into my house.

Lisa kept asking me the same questions over and over again. "When are you going to be my man? When are you going to ask me to be your woman?" She was really starting to irritate me and get on my nerves. I was so frustrated that I started hiding from her ass and moving with caution.

After months and months of Lisa chasing me, I finally gave in to her. I was getting lonely and bored playing around out in the streets, so I decided to move in with her and split the bills. The only problem was that I had a good job and she was on SSI or SSD.

Lisa had one kid, a son, and she had been getting child support from his dad, who was in the armed forces. I guess she was getting a very nice check from him because she was always very happy when those checks came in the mailbox. She would sing, "I'm in the money, I'm in the money."

"You're a fool, girl," I said, while laughing at her loony self. Then I'd give her that look—like *Are you serious?*—and walk away. I started spending lots of time with her and her son. I started loving him as if he was my own child.

A couple of months later, her sister, Vonda, was looking for a place to live. The apartment upstairs from us was empty, we told her about it and she end up getting the place.

Vonda was okay, but she seemed a little sneaky. Once she moved in upstairs, that broad would blast her music all night. I knew she would be a problem. I tolerated her because she was Lisa's older sister, but I hated the fact that she played her music all night. Vonda had a lot of company over, too. Men and women were always coming and going, and I wondered if she was selling drugs or something. It was just so crazy to me.

Five months into my relationship with Lisa, things started getting a little rocky and the tension started building. I didn't know what was causing the tension, between us because I knew it wasn't me. One day I was walking down the stairs on my way to work and some tall guy with a medium build, brown-skinned with braids in his hair, walked by me. He was heading upstairs as I was heading downstairs. I figured that Vonda had finally found a new boyfriend.

Every day we would pass each other as I left for work, and not once did this guy look me in the face or speak to me. I thought that was very odd because I am a people person who will talk to anyone. So one day I tried to be the bigger man and said, "How are you doing, man?" He just kept on walking by like he hadn't heard me. I thought, *Damn, this guy is rude as hell.* So I never spoke to him again. Every morning I walked by and didn't even look his way. Something seemed fishy about this guy.

One day after a hard day's work I came home, showered, and got dressed. Lisa sat beside me with a very sad look on her face and said, "Lenny, I'm not happy with our relationship."

"Where the hell did that come from?" I asked, surprised and a little angry. I got up and started pacing the floor in the apartment. Then I walked by the bedroom and saw a condom wrapper on the floor. It was close to the bed, nearly under it. Lisa and I were having unprotected sex at the time, so I was hurt when I saw that. I yelled loudly, almost screaming, "What the hell is this, Lisa? Are you cheating on me?!"

"No, no, I'm not cheating. I'm just not happy," she said, with a shocked look on her face. At that moment her expression changed and her skin went pale. "Maybe my sister dropped that. You know she's down here all the time." She was nervous and seemed to be lying.

"Your sister has her own apartment, so why would she drop that here? That's bullshit!" I said loudly. I was so upset. I walked into the bathroom and saw a small bullet in the toilet. I yelled, "What the hell is this?"

Lisa began to cry harder and harder, and all I could do was look at her in disbelief. She looked me dead in my eyes and said, "I just can't be with you anymore, Lenny."

I kept asking her question after question and wouldn't let up. "Why, Lisa, why?"

"I'm seeing someone else. He said he would kill you if I didn't break up with you."

"Oh, that's why that bullet is in the toilet?" I asked.

"He must have left it there, but I didn't see him do that," she said with intensity.

"How did it get that far, Lisa, where he could make you choose him, girl? I was a good man to you, so why would you do that to me?" I asked. My voice was trembling and there were tears in my eyes. I was so hurt, I could hardly talk correctly. I kept stuttering.

Lisa was now weeping and frowning as I talked to her. She couldn't take any more of my questioning and just walked out on me. She headed upstairs to her sister's apartment.

I sat on the couch in shock and prayed to God. I was breathing heavily. At that moment I was so angry that I tore up the whole house. I opened the windows, and the wind blew in cold air. I shot clothes everywhere, shot dishes to the floor. The living room looked like Hurricane Katrina had come through. I was really pissed.

When Lisa returned from upstairs, she was in shock and pissed at the same damn time. I was livid, so I grabbed all my clothes, which I had stuffed in big plastic bags, and told her ass, "Good luck, Lisa, because I'm out of here."

She cried louder and louder as I carried my bags out the door. I couldn't believe I had been hurt again in another relationship. I felt so betrayed. *Why would she do this to me?* I asked myself. She knew I had been hurt like this in the past, because we had many conversations about how much drama I had gone through with other women. I just couldn't understand it. I was totally at a loss to explain her actions.

That night, after driving around for hours in my car thinking about what had happened, I decided to stay with my mother for the night. What would I do now? Where would I go from here?

The next morning I woke up and decided to stake out Lisa's house like I was a detective, just to see if she would walk out with this guy, whose name was Tone. I waited patiently, and at about 9 a.m. Lisa walked out. Not even three seconds later, Tone walked out too. My face turned red, and I was so filled with anger that I was practically blowing smoke. I was shocked to see them holding hands as they walked down the street. Tone was the guy who had passed me on the stairs for a while now as I was heading out to work. "Damn, not the guy who wouldn't speak to me," I said to myself.

I was a fool, a big damn fool, I had been. They had played me. It kept running through my mind. I was so irate that I knew I was going to get revenge on their asses.

Not even two weeks later, Tone dumped Lisa. She came back to me, crying and begging, while I was at my cousin's house. I made her crawl on the floor—yes, on her hands and knees. She crawled in the front door and up the stairs in front of all my cousins and friends, apologizing like she had stolen something from a store and gotten caught. I acted like I forgave her and led her upstairs. We had sex, and afterward I told her, "Hell no! I don't want you back, and I do not accept your apology." I said it loudly enough so that everybody in the house could hear that shit. Then I made her trifling ass leave the house.

Chapter Six

Keisha

The day after I made Lisa leave my cousin's house, I went to the breakfast restaurant to get something to eat from the drive-thru. I heard a nice voice on the intercom. As I pulled up, I saw a nice cutie. She was a sexy little thing. I had seen her before in passing awhile back, so I was surprised to see her working at the restaurant.

"Isn't your name Tim?" she asked.

"No, it's not."

"Yes it is, yes it is."

"Sorry, but you've got the wrong guy. Anyway, what's your name?" I asked.

"My name is Keisha," she said with a big smile on her cute little face.

I was holding up the line while other customers wanted to order. I didn't care about that, though, because I was talking to this sexy momma. I was determined to get Lisa out of my system for good. "I get off work at ten thirty tonight," she said.

"Do you want me to come back and pick you up, Keisha?" I asked smoothly. "Do you need a ride? I can come back and get you."

She stared at me for a second and paused, as if she was trying to see whether or not I was serious. After that short stare, she smiled and asked, "Are you coming back for real?"

"I promise I will," I replied with a big grin on my face.

I could see her still smiling as I pulled away, the other customers still blowing their horns at me. I just laughed even more loudly because I knew I had just pissed them off. I didn't care, because this little cutie named Keisha had to be mine. I mean, this girl was as sexy as a runway model—no lie. She stayed on my mind all day. She was ten times better-looking than Lisa, so I knew I had me a winner.

I kept looking at my watch, and whatever I was doing that day, I would sometimes stop and look at the clock also. It seemed as if ten o'clock took forever to come. I was so anxious. I got in my car and headed back to the restaurant to pick Keisha up as I had promised her earlier.

When I walked into the lobby of the restaurant, I didn't see Keisha at first. I thought she had left already, maybe because she thought I wasn't serious about coming to pick her up. Finally, after about ten minutes of waiting and looking, she came out from the back. I was happy, so I smiled.

When Keisha got in the car, my eyes lit up; I was grinning from ear to ear. "I don't even know your name since it's not Tim," she said with a little chuckle. "So are you going to tell me?"

"My, my name is Lenny," I said nervously. Quickly my nervousness changed to confidence as we began engaging in more conversation. "So who is this Tim guy? You must have really liked him," I joked.

Keisha started shaking her head. "Well, we were only friends, and you look so much alike. Lenny, I'm sorry, honey," she said softly.

"That's all right. I understand when someone has made an impression in your life." There was silence for a moment. Then we began to stare at each other and smile.

Keisha told me she lived on the northwest side of town. As I got closer to her house, I was thinking to myself, *I like this girl, and I wish I didn't have to take her home.*

She saw the smile on my face and asked, "What are you smiling about?"

I laughed and said, "I wish you didn't have to go home, that's all."

"Yeah, I know, but I have to be right back up to do a double." I like a hardworking woman, so I understood. She told me she didn't have any kids either. That was a plus. "Okay, maybe this weekend we can go on a date?" she asked.

"Sure, that will be nice."

As the weekend got closer, Keisha and I stayed on the phone all night. We talked about a lot that entire week. I picked her up from work a couple of times that week. When Friday came, I picked her up again.

"Can you take me to the check cashing place so I can cash my check?" she asked as she sat down in the car.

"Sure, which one?" I said. She said the one by her house would be okay, so we went there. After cashing her check, Keisha wanted to go to the mall. I took her there, and she asked me if I wanted this or that. Like the gentleman I am, I said with a smile, "Sure." She bought me an outfit and some cologne. *Wow, this is a good woman*, I thought. I almost said it out loud but caught myself. With bags in hand, we headed out of the mall.

As we put the bags in the car, I asked Keisha, "Why don't you have a boyfriend? You are such a nice young woman."

"I was talking to someone, but he's incarcerated for a year or so."

"Oh, are you still in contact with him?" I asked, my forehead wrinkled.

"I'm not going to lie. Yes, I am."

"Oh wow," I said with my mouth open. "When he gets out, will you go back to him?"

"I don't really know. It's been a long time since we've been together and a lot has changed."

"Well, please let me know before I get my feelings in too deep."

Keisha looked in my eyes and said, "Okay, I will let you know."

Even though she was honest with me, the relationship she had with this guy in jail bothered me. The thought stayed in the back of my mind like a thorn in my side. I talked to her about it, but she said I didn't have anything to worry about. I just shook my head in disbelief. *Yeah, right.*

We started going on dates and really enjoying each other. Then one day I said, "So, Keisha, when is your so-called man supposed to be getting out of jail?"

She paused for a second and said, "His sister said he will be out sometime next week."

"Next week?" I exclaimed. "Oh, so you and his sister are cool like that."

Keisha said nervously, "Yeah. Yes, we are."

I thought to myself, *Damn, I wonder if she would have told me that if I hadn't asked her.* Then I gave her a surprised look. "So what's his name?" I asked with a curious but stern look on my face.

"His name is CJ."

At that moment I had a lot on my mind, and I started sweating profusely. She started rubbing my hands as if to comfort me. I was thinking to myself that next week was coming fast. Would she leave me or would she go back to him? These questions ran through my head like speedboats. They really frustrated me. I let her know exactly how I felt about the situation. All I got from her was a glassy-eyed stare as if the cat got her tongue.

The weekend finally came and Keisha did not leave my side. I still remember. It was a very hot, sticky day, so I decided to take her down to the pier on the beach. We began holding hands as we hit the pier, which was crowded with people. It seemed as if everybody was a couple and holding hands.

When we got to the end of the pier, Keisha started crying—I mean, crocodile tears just started rolling. I asked, "What's wrong and why are you crying, hon?"

For a while she just couldn't stop crying, and then her nose started running. At that moment I felt so bad because I didn't know what was wrong with her. Then she sniffled, "I don't know what to do, Lenny. I love CJ and I am falling in love with you at the same time."

I held her close to me very tightly and said, "You have to do what's best for you. You are the only woman who was honest with me from the start."

"Well, I had to be. My mother always said, 'Treat others like you want to be treated.'"

We started walking back to the beach from the pier. We held each other very firmly, and I didn't want to let her go. I didn't know whether or not this would be the last time I held her, so I held on as if it was for dear life. We headed back to the car and just sat there for a little while.

The next day came and I didn't hear from Keisha. I called her and left many messages, but there was no response. I couldn't understand why she wasn't answering my phone calls. I hadn't done anything wrong for her to be acting this way toward me. I was so bored that day, and my stomach felt unsettled. Questions like, *Where is she?* and *What could she be doing?* raced through my mind.

I went into my room and started searching for old movies to put in the DVD player. Then I got bored again and started playing my video game. I was very distraught. I didn't know what to do or what to think. I was a complete mess. Every time my phone rang, I would race to the phone, but it wasn't her. I walked outside and stared at the sky. That day there wasn't a cloud in it. The sun was shining, and it seemed as if everything had gone still.

As it began to get dark outside, I realized that I wouldn't hear from Keisha today. I couldn't eat or sleep. I stayed up most of the night on my computer. I put my lamp on low and tried sleeping a few times, but she was too much on my mind.

My head started hurting, so I took some Advil. I needed something for my headache because the stress was just killing me. After the migraine slowly faded, I fell asleep around 4 a.m. I tossed and turned throughout the night. It wasn't a good sleep at all.

Two days went by and I still hadn't heard from or seen Keisha. I was starting to get very worried. All my calls and messages were going unanswered. I rode down her street several times to see if she was sitting outside, but nothing.

I didn't want it to seem like I was stalking her, but in a sense I was. I was not trying to go out like that—uh-uh, no way. As I drove around in my car, I saw one of Keisha's friends, Meloney Howard, going into the store, so I stopped. Meloney would know something. I yelled, "Meloney, Meloney!"

She stopped and said, "Who is that calling me? Oh, hey, Lenny. What's up?"

I said, "What's up with your friend, Keisha? Is she okay? I haven't talked to her or seen her in a couple of days. Have you seen her?"

"Yes, I just saw her yesterday, and she was telling me CJ is getting out of jail—I think she said tomorrow," she said with an intense look on her face.

"I wonder why she didn't tell me. She won't answer my calls, so I don't know what's going on with her."

"I'm sorry to tell you this, Lenny, but she's in love with that loser. He keeps going in and out of jail. He's no good for her, but she doesn't see that. I know she cares about you 'cause she told me so, but she just doesn't want to hurt your feelings."

After our little conversation Meloney went in the store and I went to the car and sat for a while, thinking that I had to see Keisha before CJ got out. I pulled into traffic slowly, rode a few blocks, and stopped at the convenient store to buy a beer. The wheels in my head were spinning. *I've got to see her, I've got to see her* kept repeating in the back of my head like a whisper. So I got the courage to go by her house after I gulped down the beer.

I got out of the car and walked up to the door, hesitant to knock. Finally I did—*knock, knock, knock.*

Some guy came to the door and told me come in. I didn't know who he was, but I thought maybe he was a relative. Six guys were standing around looking angry, and Keisha was in her bedroom doing her friend's hair.

When Keisha saw me, she was shocked and started waving her hand as if to say, *Don't say your here for me.* But I didn't know anyone in the house but her.

Then one of the guys stepped to me and said, "I'm CJ. Who are you here for?"

I didn't know what to say since Keisha was in the other room. I could see her moving her lips quietly, while talking and making gestures. *Not me, not me*, she said

He said again with a deep voice, "Who are you here for?"

Then I got the nerve and asked, "What's it to you?" puffing my chest out.

CJ got a little angrier when I asked that question. He shouted, "I'm asking you because Keisha is my girl!" Then he pulled a shiny gun from his pocket.

My eyes grew big and my heart started racing. I couldn't even speak. Then I heard Keisha say, "No, I'm not your woman."

One of the guys CJ was with said, "That's messed up, man. See, you can't trust a woman." I guess he was trying to make the situation worse.

CJ ran into Keisha's room and hit her in the head with the gun. I saw that and, just for that split second as everybody turned to look at what CJ was doing, I ran to the door and unlocked the three locks so fast.

I jumped over the steps and ran. I heard CJ and his friends yelling, "He's getting away! Catch him." Then I heard a gun pop. *Pop, pop, pop!* rang out like a firecracker. I ran frantically. I couldn't believe this guy was shooting at me, and that he had just hit Keisha with that gun. It just blew me away. I tried to jump up on the curb, blew my back out when I missed the curb, and stumbled.

I got to my street and ran into my neighbor, Terrell. He said, "What's wrong, Lenny?"

I said, "This fool named CJ shot at me over his girl."

"Do you want to get him, Lenny?" Terrell offered, looking serious.

"Do you have a gun?"

"No."

"Hell no. I'm not going back if you don't have a gun."

About a week later, I heard CJ had been found murdered. People said he had drugs stuck in his underwear near his privates. I never had a chance to get back at him. I guess the man upstairs took care of that.

It was three months before I saw Keisha again. When I saw her she was smiling. I looked at her as if to say, *What the hell are you smiling at?*

We started talking and decided to part as friends, no hard feelings. She told me a little bit about what had happened to CJ, but I wasn't listening. I said good-bye and told her to take care of herself. We hugged and that was it. As I walked away, I took a deep breath. I knew I had just escaped death.

Part Two

Richard's Story

Chapter One

Petey, Cynthia, Tabby, and Shara

Hi, I'm Richard and I remember when I was in puppy love with this girl named Cynthia. She was very fine, with a pecan complexion and a beautiful smile. Cynthia and her family had just moved down the street from me. As soon as I saw her, my eyes lit up like street-lights. She would always smile at me, so one day I got up the nerve to ask her to be my girlfriend and she accepted.

Cynthia asked me in a sultry, soft voice, "Am I your only girl-friend, Richard?"

Shaking, I answered, "Yes, you are, baby. What about yourself, Cynthia?"

She said, "No, I don't have any girlfriends." Then she started laughing.

"You know what I'm saying, smarty pants. Am I your only boy-friend?"

Cynthia said, "Yes, you are my only boyfriend."

We did a lot of things together, like going to dinner and to the movies, and walking in the parks. We both were romantics and loved showing affection in public. I introduced her to my family and met hers. They were a really tight-knit family, unlike mine.

I called them my second family. If you saw her, then you would see me. She was my best friend. I would talk to my friends about her and they would get jealous because they were single and alone.

My friend Danny swore that she was a whore who would cheat on me one day. I told him off. I said a whole bunch of stuff, but the last thing I remember saying is, "My girl won't ever cheat on me."

He said, "Okay, okay, just watch and see."

I told him to kiss my ass, and then I left. Why was he hating on me?

I never told Cynthia what my friends were saying. I was steaming, but they had their own opinions. I knew deep down I was right. I mean, why would she cheat on me? I was so good to her, and she was good to me too. We bought each other things we wanted for our birthdays and everything.

Then one day we were sitting on her porch and saw a very big moving truck pull up. An elderly woman, older gentleman, young guy, and girl hopped out of the truck. They had so much stuff and they moved all day until the evening. Cynthia and I started walking down the street, and as we were going to the store, the young guy spoke and said, "Hi, my name is Petey."

Then he asked us our names, so I said, "Hi, I'm Richard, and this is my girlfriend Cynthia." He was very funny and started joking. He had us laughing right off the bat.

So every day after work, we would hang out. Then one day I got a call for a job; they offered me a position at Perkins Restaurant. I was ecstatic. I told Cynthia, "Baby, I just got a job offer."

Cynthia didn't seem as happy as I was. She said, with her head down, "We won't be able spend time together anymore." I assured her that we would. The job was nice, and I began to work more hours than expected. Cynthia would argue with me about it. I told her I had to work in order to make a living.

I told her, "If a man doesn't work, then a man doesn't eat." This only made her angrier. Then she started calling less and less often. I asked her why and she said she was giving me space because my job was more important than she was. That really pissed me off. Why couldn't she understand that I had to work? Why wouldn't she get a job? Maybe she wouldn't be so lonely. Maybe it would keep her from talking junk to me about working.

One evening I got off late and saw her sitting on Petey's steps. I walked up slowly and asked what they were up to. They both answered, "Nothing." That didn't sit well with me, but I didn't make a big deal about it. I trusted Cynthia, so there wasn't a reason to get upset. My thoughts were only on the two of us and our future.

Day by day she was getting colder and colder. So I sat her down and asked her with a very concerned look on my face, "Baby, what's the matter? Am I not making you happy?"

She just shook her head and said in a low voice, "I'm all right, I'm all right."

I tried to tell her that she was my future and that this job was a stepping stone. I had plans to go back to school, so that in the future I could take care of us both. She wasn't hearing it; instead she started talking about all the times we had spent together. She said that we really didn't see each other much and she got lonely sometimes. So I went to work and asked my boss to cut my hours a little, and he did.

That night I didn't tell Cynthia I was getting off work early. When I came down the street, I saw Cynthia and Petey walking very close toward her house. I guess they saw the headlights shining because they hurried up and separated. Petey looked back and must have whispered something to her like, "That might be Richard, so we'd better move apart before he sees us walking close."

Well, that was the way I took it anyway. They had separated fast when the headlights showed up. I pulled up slowly, and said to them both with a funny smirk on my face, "What's going on?"

Looking very sneaky, they both said, "Nothing."

I told Cynthia to get in the car so that we could talk. Petey just watched as she got into my car.

Once she was in my car, I started asking her, "What the hell is going on?" I was looking very serious at this point.

"What are you talking about?" she asked.

"You know what I'm talking about. Every time I pull up, I see you and Petey walking together."

"Nothing. He's just been keeping me company while you're working so much," she said in a slick tone.

"Well, it looks like more than that to me."

"There's nothing going on."

My jealousy rate went sky-high, but she stuck to her story that they were only friends. I felt like Petey was up too something, though; I could feel it in my bones. So I stopped badgering Cynthia about it and tried to just trust her. But I still saw them together pretty often after work. So one day I pulled Petey aside and asked him, man to man, "Are you trying to steal my girl, man?"

He laughed. "No, man, we're just friends and that's all."

For some reason the way he said it and the expression on his face didn't sit well with me, but I let it go because my issue was with her, not him.

One Wednesday night our neighbor Miss Randle yelled out to me, "Hey, *pssssst*. Hey, Richard." She lowered her voice. "I've been seeing your girlfriend with—what's that young new guy's name?—Pete something. I saw them all hugged up and holding hands on the side of the house. I don't know what they were doing."

"You mean Petey and Cynthia," I said with jealousy and hurt in my heart. As I walked away, Miss Randle said in a wise but caring tone, "Just watch for yourself—don't just listen to me."

When I got halfway down the block, Mr. Hathaway called out to me in a deep voice. "Richard, Richard, come here. Come h-h-h-h-h-here." He talked with a stutter. It sounded so funny, but I couldn't laugh because I was so upset about what Miss Randle had told me about Cynthia and Petey.

"I, I, I, think, think, think, I saw your, your girlfriend kissing that new g-g-g-g-guy." It took Mr. Hathaway almost fifteen minutes to get that one out.

I was steaming and hurt. I couldn't believe what I was hearing. So I waited until the next day and asked Cynthia about it, and she denied it all. She said I was trying to start stuff and turned it around on me, blaming me for not spending time with her and saying I was more about work than about her. I remembered what Miss Randle had said and decided to find out for myself.

Weeks and weeks went by and I couldn't find anything, but everyone kept telling me these juicy tales of Cynthia and Petey messing around behind my back. I knew it was a matter of time before the truth would come out. So I told Cynthia I had to work that Thursday, but I didn't really have to go in. I parked at the end of the street and just waited. It was dark and the moon was out. Then I saw a porch light come on at Cynthia's house. She came out on the porch and started looking around, staring down the street toward Petey's house. Then the light came on at his house and he came out, looking around. I think she called his name, because all of a sudden, he noticed her and started walking her way. They had no clue I was there hiding in the car. I was like a detective in the movies, just watching.

They met each other and kissed. Now I was livid. His arms wrapped around her like she was his woman. A part of me wanted to confront them, but I didn't; I just kept watching. Then I saw them at the side of the house.

I got out of my car and starting tiptoeing down the street quietly. I couldn't see them from the side of the house, so I decided to go all the way to the back. As I approached I heard some light breathing, and when I turned the corner at the back of the house—boy, was there a surprise for me.

Petey had Cynthia bent over and they were having sex. I couldn't believe what I was seeing, I thought I was in a very bad dream, but it wasn't funny. I watched for a second, and then they must have sensed me there because Petey turned around and looked at me like he had seen a ghost.

When Cynthia turned, tears rolled down her face. She began saying over and over, "I'm sorry, I'm sorry, I'm sorry." She started pulling up her panties and clothes.

I walked away, tears rolling down my cheeks, and she started walking behind me. I was crying like I had just lost my best friend. "How could you do this to me?" I said in a rage. I was spitting while talking and my hands were shaking badly. "I thought I meant something to you." It occurred to me that I should've kicked Petey's ass, but I realized it took two to tango, so I let him live that day. I knew that I was going to get him back some way and somehow. "Do you love him?" I asked.

"No, no, I swear I don't. Plus the sex wasn't any good anyway."

I said loudly. "What? That doesn't matter. Was that supposed to make me feel better?"

Cynthia said, "I was lonely and you weren't here. You started working so much and forgot about me."

"Are you serious, Cynthia? That is no damn excuse. I don't know if I can ever forgive you or trust you now." That night we talked in the car till the sun started rising. Cynthia tried to explain, but I wasn't listening. We both cried very hard. I let her know that we couldn't be a couple anymore because I couldn't trust her. She wouldn't let it go. She would call me every hour of every day.

One weekend Cynthia's friend Tabby came to my job at the restaurant. I went on break and Tabby started talking about how Cynthia had really messed up a good thing with me. Then she started coming to my job every other day or so to chat with me. We talked about hanging out on the weekends. Even though I knew she was Cynthia's friend, I didn't feel it was a wrong thing to do.

Friday came and we planned to meet up after work, so I met her at the movie theater in the parking lot. She was dressed up really nicely and smelled good. Wow! So we went to this bar on the West Side and started having drinks and talking and laughing. Then we started bar hopping. We were really having a good time. We were so drunk that neither of us could drive. There was a hotel nearby, so we decided to stay there until the morning. We got a room and I lay on the bed while she got in the shower.

Then she came out of the bathroom with a towel on. Her body was glistening and those curves were, like, *oooowee*! I went to the bathroom to shower, too. When I came out Tabby was laying on the bed naked. I lay down on the bed next to her. She started rubbing on me and kissing me softly all over. Then her head went down slowly between my legs and she began giving me the best oral sex I had ever had. Then we started having passionate sex. I couldn't believe it was happening, but I was like, *Damn, this feels so good.* I mean, we went at it until we both passed out. The next morning when I woke up, I couldn't believe what had happened. We both agreed not to tell anyone and that we would just remain friends. I knew if Cynthia found about Tabby and me she would be hurt.

Tabby and I started creeping around all the time. She would actually sneak down after hanging out with Cynthia. Then one day she told me that she was moving out of town with her parents. She said they were moving south. I kissed her and told her to keep in touch because I would go down to visit.

Just like that, Tabby was gone. A little while after that, I noticed Petey's little sister, Shara, staring at me when I would pull up the street to go in the house. She was three years younger than I was, but she was nice. One day she finally got the courage to talk to me. She didn't know anything about Cynthia cheating on me with her brother, and I wasn't about to tell her either. She said she had always had a crush on me, but didn't think I liked her because she was younger. I told her I had a little crush on her, but I wasn't going to talk to her first.

We both laughed. I gave her my number and she gave me hers. I called and talked to her for a long time on the phone. She had a good sense of humor, so she kept me laughing. She had an old soul, very mature for her age. Shara told me that she was a virgin and that she wanted me to be her first. It shocked me at first, but I was like, "Okay, cool." So I got a hotel room and picked her up at the corner of our street, where no one would notice us.

I was very gentle with her. She held me so tight. I thought to myself for a second, *Damn, I'm getting Petey back.* That was only a quick thought, though. After that night Shara loved me to death. I hated the fact that we had to always sneak around. One day I told her I just wanted to be friends and that she should talk to someone her age. I thought I was doing the right thing, but she burst into tears and cried so hard that it made tears come to my eyes. I realized that she cared about me a lot and I was breaking her heart. It didn't feel good.

I thought I was getting back at Petey, but I guess I wasn't. Instead I was breaking a young girl's heart. I felt very selfish. From that day on, Shara wouldn't speak to me or even look my way. I understood, though, and hoped one day things would be better between us.

I had just wanted Cynthia and Petey to pay for their betrayal, but I realized they didn't know I had gotten them back. So I set out to do some soul searching. I vowed not to get in another relationship for a while—at least, that's what I thought.

Chapter Two

Dominique and Leon

One day I went to work and saw a couple of guys and girls getting hired by my supervisor. There was a short girl with dark skin and a light-skinned one of average height. The two guys were hired as busboys and the two girls were hired as waitresses.

My supervisor introduced them to our crew. I noticed the light-skinned girl eyeing me up and down. During the break she introduced herself to me.

"Hi, I'm Dominique. How are you doing?" she said with a blaze in her eye.

I smiled and said, "My name is Richard."

Dominique started asking me a whole slew of questions about the job. "How long have you worked here? Do you like it here?"

"I've been here almost a year now, and it's a fairly good job," I said with a smirk.

After that day no one could keep us apart. We would take breaks and lunch together. Sometimes when her ride didn't show up, I would take her home. Dominique was single and so was I. Sometimes we would talk about getting in a relationship, but we both were scared. After talking for a while, we decided to make it official.

The very first time we made love, I was supposed to pull out, but it was so good that I couldn't and Dominique got pregnant. I was so upset with myself, but at the same time this was my first child and I hoped it would be a boy.

Dominique was scared and excited because this was her first child too. "I want to have a girl," she said.

"No, I want to have a boy and no girls," I said seriously.

Dominique looked at me and chuckled. "We'll see."

The time was near for Dominique to have the baby, and she had to do an ultrasound. I went with her that day, and the doctor said it was a baby boy. I was so happy and relieved that it wasn't a girl. Even though Dominique had wanted a girl, she was still happy. We said we would name him RJ (Richard Junior).

Then the time came for the baby to be born. I got the call while I was at work; Dominique was now on maternity leave. I had to walk with her to help her have the baby faster. RJ was born and I was so happy. After the baby was born, Dominique and I didn't spend as much time together anymore. It was all about the baby now with her. I tried to talk with her about it but didn't really get a response, so I started hanging out with my boy Leon. I had met Leon at the neighborhood basketball court, and after that we became best friends.

Dominique starting having problems because I was hanging out with Leon all the time. I told her that she was always busy with the baby and didn't have time for me anymore. I just ignored her and went about my business. Leon would always try to hook me up with women and try doing double dates. I would tell him," I'm not doing that—that's your thing." He would laugh and tease me, saying I was sprung out.

"Yup, whatever you say," I would say. I wasn't falling for his little games, so I didn't pay him any attention. "You do you and I will do me," I said with a wise attitude.

He just waved his hand at me as if to say, *Man, shut up!*

Every night I came home late, Dominique would be up waiting for me and would start badgering me and making me upset. I told her, "Whenever I try to spend time with you, you always have something planned with the baby."

She just looked at me and shook her head. "Ooooh, I can't stand it anymore, you're always hanging out with Leon and not me! What are you all doing out this late anyway?"

"Just drinking at the bar, hanging out," I said with a frown on my face.

She got up, muttering under her breath. I couldn't make out what she was saying.

The arguing and nagging went on for months and months. I was getting tired of hearing it, so I started staying away from home more and more. Leon would always set up something for us to do. There was a festival called the Caribana in Toronto, Canada, and he wanted us to go. I told Dominique that I was going. She was furious with me but just shook her head as if to say, "Okay, okay, you just go on ahead."

Leon and I went to Toronto and had a ball. All these beautiful women kept coming up to us. They would ask for our phone numbers and the room numbers to our hotels.

I admit I was tipsy from drinking, so I did give my number out and some ladies came back to our hotel, but we met them in the lobby. We went out to some clubs and everybody came back to our room and crashed. The next morning I felt so guilty. Even though I hadn't crossed the line and had sex with anyone, it still felt wrong. Leon promised me that he wouldn't mention what had happened in Toronto to anyone.

When we got back home, Dominique acted cold for weeks. I tried my best to talk to her and set up things for us to do. She would just shoot down my plans. Then one day I came home from work, and she said that she was quitting her job. I said, "Quitting your job to do what?"

"For what?" she said. "I'm quitting my job to get on social services."

I said loudly, "The hell you are."

One day I came home from work to find her cooking. I said, "Why aren't you going to work?"

She stared and me and said, "I quit, that's why."

I was so upset that I just threw my jacket off and went to vent in the basement. I could not believe it that she was serious about leaving her job to live on the county.

From then on I had to take care of her and the baby financially, and it was hard. That load was so heavy on my shoulders, and I was constantly stressed out. When I told Leon, he laughed and shrugged his shoulders.

One day I came home after work and Dominique was on the phone laughing out loud. I didn't bother her; I took my shower and sat on the couch watching TV. She was walking in and out of rooms while cooking. She was so tickled, and I hadn't seen her like this in a while. I was thinking it must be somebody in her family tripping that had her cracking up like that. Everyone in her family was a comedian and very entertaining.

After about half an hour, she handed me the phone. I was shocked to hear the voice on the other end—it was my boy Leon. I thought she didn't like Leon. All this time they'd been laughing and talking while I was just sitting there. I was so pissed off that I hung up on his ass.

The next day when I saw Leon, I told him. "Don't ever call my house and talk to my girl. If I'm not there, just hang up."

Trying to plead his case, he said, "I thought we were all cool like family."

"Not with my damn girl you're not."

Before he could open his mouth, I scooped him up in the air on my shoulder. I told him, "I will hurt you if you do it again." Then I set him down on his feet.

After that I didn't see much of Leon. We would see each other out and about and would just wave or give the peace sign. Things with Dominique and I weren't the same either. We were barely even sleeping together anymore. I told her ass off about the phone call with Leon, and that killed most of our communication around the house. I couldn't understand why she would converse with him, especially when she acted like she hated his guts.

I started noticing that when I came home from work, Dominique would hang up the phone as soon as I opened the door. I tried not to let it bother me, but it just kept happening and I was starting to get frustrated. So I asked her in a deep voice, "Who are you on the phone with? It had better be one of your girlfriends."

She just looked me, and then turned around and went in the other room. I couldn't believe that I was getting a little jealous, but I was.

Then one day Dominique suddenly started asking me questions about places and people I knew. The questions she was asking were about things only a couple of my friends knew. I couldn't understand how she knew to ask me these things. It never dawned on me that someone was telling her my personal stuff because that went against the men's code. She wouldn't confess to where she was getting all this information, so I just ignored her when she asked.

After months and months of arguing, I decided to break up with her. This relationship was not working out at all. We still would chat on the phone because, after all, we did have a child together. Sometimes I would ride by the house just to see if the lights were on or to see if someone was home.

One Friday night in October, I rode by using the back way. I stopped fast, as if I was lead-footed. I blinked several times and thought I was seeing things. It looks like Leon's car was parked in back of Dominique's house. I even got a close-up view of the plates to make sure. Damn, I was steaming now. I wanted to blow my top. I knew I was going to kick his ass when I saw him.

I was sweating and shaking with anger; I wanted to hurt someone badly, especially if my kid was there. I went around to the front and knocked on the door forcefully. Then I began yelling, "Leon, that better not be your trifling ass at my baby momma's house!" I heard a little scuffling, then silence.

I started yelling both their names and kicking the door. I heard what sounded like a window opening in the back and then a car screeched off. I ran to the back and saw Leon car's as he hit the corner.

Dominique wouldn't open the door for anything. I called her phone—no answer. My thoughts slowly turned to Leon. I knew I had to kick his ass because he had violated our friendship in the worst way. I knew where his mom lived, so I started heading that way.

I called Leon, but he wouldn't answer his phone either. I started thinking to myself, *I thought they didn't like each other, but all along I was a damn fool.*

A tear slowly hit my right cheek, and then another came down the left cheek a little faster. At that point I didn't even care if I caught Leon in front of his whole family's house; I was going to get his ass tonight.

I pulled near Leon's mom's house and could see Mrs. Parsell out in the garden. I walked up and said, "Hi, Mrs. Parsell. Is Leon home?"

"Yeah, he just got home not long ago."

As she went back to tending the garden, I asked, "Can you call him out here? I need to talk to him."

"Leon, Leon, come outside," she yelled at the door.

When he came down to the door, I said roughly, "Sorry, Mrs. Parsell, but I have to whoop Leon's behind." I grabbed Leon from behind the door and we started going at it. He got a couple of licks in, but after that I started wailing on him good. I could hear Mrs. Parsell say, "Please don't kill my son. What did he do?"

I laid him out. He was dazed on the ground with his nose and lip bleeding. As I stood above him, I explained to her that he had been sneaking around and sleeping with my baby momma. She was shocked because she knew how close we were. She started hollering at him as she picked him up, with grass and dirt all over his head.

I got back in my car, knuckles all bloody, but I didn't feel any better. I was crushed. It took two weeks before I talked to Dominique. She cried and tried to explain, but I wasn't listening. I cursed her out so badly. I asked if our kid had been there and she denied that. If he had been, I would whoop Leon's ass again and again. After that I would not even speak to Dominique. She was now nothing to me. It seemed as if a part of me had died.

I knew somebody had to pay for this betrayal. One weekend all my fellas came over. I told them I had made a sex tape with Dominique and asked them if they wanted to see it. At this point I didn't care because I felt if she wanted to hurt me, then I was going to hurt her back.

So after we all sat down to watch, one of my fellas said, "Are you serious, man? Do you really have a video to show us?"

"Hell yeah. I don't care about her anymore. She did me dirty, so I'm going to show y'all the video. Now let the games begin," I said with a smirk on my face. That video had Dominique doing everything under the sun to me. My heart was truly cold. Maybe I shouldn't have shown them, but this was my way of making sure I wouldn't ever get back with her again. It was now time for a new chapter in my life. It was time to move on.

As for Leon, I knew his days were numbered. It was just a matter of time before I got him back for what he had done to me. He knew he had crossed the line, so he stayed hidden for a long time. I doubt he enjoyed that ass whooping I had given him in front of his mother.

Months later Dominique started calling my phone and asking me to sleep with her. I laughed and said in a deep, nasty tone, "Hell no! Stop calling my damn phone. Only call me about our kid and that's it." She wouldn't stop calling, though, so finally I decided to just go and let her perform oral sex on me. She was very good at it, so why not let her? I would just leave afterward like nothing had happened.

I guess she thought that this would change my mind and that I would get back with her, but she was sadly mistaken. I told her no over and over again. She was relentless, so finally I decided to stop letting her even touch me. I would just go over, get our son, and leave. I stayed in the car so that I wouldn't be even a little tempted.

I had to admit that her oral game was so good I would almost give in sometimes, but I had to be strong. I didn't have any intention of being with her, and I told her that over and over again.

I thought about the times I had shown that video, and that was the one thing that really let me know I could never get back with her. I wasn't really happy about the fact that she didn't know I had gotten her back by showing the video to everyone, so I didn't feel as good as I thought I would. I wanted her to hurt. Maybe one day she would know, but it was time for me to move on.

Chapter Three

My Friend Cam

After Dominique and I broke up, I stayed single for a while. I started hanging out at all the bars around town. Every Wednesday they would have "Bar Association," where all the little bars would join together and invite everyone to party at one bar. I would go in and shoot darts and play pool. The place was always flooded with women. They would stare at me and I would stare back. This was my routine every week.

They always gave me compliments on what I was wearing and what kind of cologne I had on. It always made me smile. I even started dating again, but only as friends. No one had caught my eye yet.

One weekend I ran into my friend Cam, whom I had gone to school with. We bought each other drinks and then exchanged numbers. He was a funny dude. He was always bragging about himself. We clicked well because we had a lot in common.

Cam and I would meet up every now and again to chill and check out the women. He was a cool brother to hang around with—except he always acted like he had to compete with me.

One night Cam had to work late, so I went to this little bar called Hobart. They were hosting Bar Association that Sunday.

It was so packed I could barely move around in there. I mingled with a couple of friends, and after having some drinks we started shooting darts. I was on a winning streak. No one could touch me on the dartboard that night.

Then I took a break and went to bar. Then—oh my God!—about ten women came in, and *damn* they were looking good. I went back to the dartboard and told a few friends, "Wait until you see what just came in the building." Then I laughed out loud.

As I continued my winning streak on the dartboard, five of the women came to the back where we were playing, while the other five hung out at the bar. They were checking me out as I was kicking butt in the game.

My eyes were on the thick one. She looked a little taller than I was, about five foot nine. The height difference didn't bother me, though. She smiled and stared at me, so I did the same. After a game or two more, I got the courage to go over and ask her name. "Hello, how are you doing, hon? May I ask your name?"

She said, "My name is Brandy."

Smiling, I asked, "Do you shoot darts?"

"No, I just like watching you play." Then she smiled and said playfully, "I mean, watching *y'all* play."

I laughed and then asked her, "Do you drink? Or would you like a drink?"

Brandy smiled at me and said, "Sure." After that, we conversed and exchanged numbers. It was a nice night after that. I thought I would hear from her, but I never got that call. I knew that I would see her again one day, though. She sure was sexy. From what I saw, she was wife material. Who knew what was meant to happen? That was how I thought about it.

One day Cam and I met up at this party at Club Roxy. We hit the bar and got our drinks. Then we went to the dance floor. Everyone was having a good time, and the women were looking marvelous.

Then, all of a sudden, I looked to my right and there standing with her friends was Brandy. Our eyes locked and we both smiled.

I wanted to ask her why I hadn't heard from her, but I didn't. I said to Cam, "See that girl right there, the really thick pretty one? I was trying to talk her one night at Bar Association."

"What happened with that?" Cam asked. Then he smiled and said with a laugh, "Oh, I know her—well, I mean I know her cousin. He works at the barbershop. I wanted to talk to her to at one time."

I turned to tell him that I had given her my number before, but he was gone. He went over to Brandy, gave her his business card, and started talking to her. I thought, *What the hell?* I played it off as if it didn't bother me, though. When he came back over, I asked, "What'd she say?"

"Oh, she said she would call me. I told you, I know her cousin," Cam said. I thought that was wrong of him to do, especially when I had just told him I had tried to talk to her before. He acted as if he hadn't done anything wrong, so I didn't say anything.

I went to the bar and got a drink, and then just chilled around the bar. I stood by some ladies who started telling me how good I smelled. They kept me smiling. I offered to buy them drinks and they accepted. They said I was handsome and a gentleman.

As I was talking to the ladies, Cam walked up beside me. He started talking loudly, and it looked like he was turning the women off. I just shook my head.

Then we walked away and I told the ladies that I would be back over. Cam started bragging about what he was going to do to Brandy in bed. I just looked at him and shook my head.

I went to the bathroom and came back out before it was time to go, and I said good-bye to the ladies I had bought the drinks for. There was one girl standing there, and she said, "You're not going to leave your number?"

I smiled and asked her name. She said, "My name is Cindy."

We exchanged numbers and I left. Cam went his way and I went my way. As I was going to pull off, I saw Cindy waving at me and smiling, so I waved back. Then I called her number to make sure it was the right number. She answered and said, "Oh, you thought I gave you the wrong number, huh?"

I laughed. "Just checking. Okay, call you tomorrow."

I drove home thinking about what Cam had done. I couldn't believe that. I thought he was my friend, so why would he pull something like that? I knew I had to let it go, though, because it wasn't like she was my girlfriend before.

After that night Cam would tell me all about him and Brandy and how he tore her up in bed sexually. He sure was bragging a lot. Then he started taking her out to all the spots where we hung out. I wasn't seeing him as much as I used to because he was always with her. I think he was falling in love.

One morning I woke up with a missed call on my phone, and Cam's name came up in my contacts. He had left a message. I listened to my voice mail and heard a woman's voice. They were having sex. It was Brandy making noises and breathing heavily, and I could hear Cam's voice saying, "Who's your daddy now?"

I hurried up and erased the message. This guy was really starting to be an asshole. I couldn't believe he would do that. I cursed him out good later on that day, but he just laughed and joked around.

Later that night I received a call from Cindy. We chatted for a while and decided to meet somewhere for dinner. We met at a nice restaurant and had a nice time. She was pretty nice. I thought she was taller when I saw her in the club, but it must have been those six-inch heels she had on. I asked her, "How tall are you?"

"I'm only five feet."

"Wow, I thought you were taller, but I like the fact that you are a shorty." We both laughed. I told her I was enjoying our date and conversation and that I hoped we would do it again. She agreed.

Cam called me the next morning to tell me that Brandy had offered to sell some purses and watches for him. (That was his hustle on the side.) I just listened. He said she had a lot of friends that she could get to buy his stuff. I was really in shock because he never trusted anybody with his stuff. That fool was falling in love and didn't even know it.

One day Cam called and asked me if I wanted to go on a double date with him and Brandy. I started to say hell no, but I told him I'd go and that I would take this new girl named Cindy with me.

I called Cindy and asked her, and she said she would go. Cam wanted to go up to a new club in Buffalo, New York, so we made reservations and got rooms near each other in the hotel.

We went out to this nice club called Sensations. It was a nice crowd, and we all had a great time. When we got to our rooms it was on, especially after drinking some alcohol. Cindy and I made love all over that room. It was what I needed.

Next morning Cam met me in the lounge on the way to breakfast, and he was bragging about what he had done to Brandy in bed. I just laughed.

It was a nice weekend, I must admit, even though my so-called friend was a jerk.

A few months went by after that, and then Cam called me and said, "I think Brandy and I are going to get married next year, sometime around August."

"What? Come on, man. You haven't even known her long enough to be talking about marriage," I teased. "You must be sprung, dude."

"No, I'm not. Who puts a time on something like that anyway?" he said. I couldn't stop laughing because she had his ass and he didn't even know it. He was supposed to be so hard that a woman couldn't get to him. Whatever!

I hung up on him while he was still explaining his side. *He's a dummy*, I thought, *and he will find out.* I laughed even harder.

I was at work one day when Cam called me. He sounded frantic and upset. I asked what was going on and he told me Brandy had looked in his closet and found letters from his ex. He tried to tell her that they were letters, but she didn't believe him. I knew he was telling the truth because he told me everything, but she wasn't buying it.

I asked him, "How did she get in your closet, man?"

"Oh, I didn't tell you, but Brandy had to move out of her place, and she asked me if she could stay here until she found a place."

I exclaimed, "What? Are you kidding, man? When did this happen, Cam?"

"It happened Monday."

I was shocked to hear that news. It came as a big surprise. Now Brandy always acted jealous and didn't trust him. She didn't know that he really did care about her. I thought, *Wow, I didn't have to do anything to get him back. That's exactly what happens when you do underhanded stuff like he did to me.* He was getting exactly what he deserved.

A few weeks later he called me and told me that she kept accusing him of cheating. She had found some nude pictures of some of his old girlfriends. He tried to tell her they were old, but now her guard was up. All I knew was that Cam sounded really upset and hurt because he really liked Brandy and was ready to settle down with her. I knew he was serious when he said that he wanted to get married to her after only a few months of knowing her, and now he had moved her into his house.

Now they were arguing every other day, and he would call me trying to get advice from me. I really couldn't tell him anything. Now I was glad I'd never talked to her. He said she was snooping in all his stuff. Every day she had something to say about the letters and pictures she had found. He told me she asked him why he still had them if they are an old ex's. His crazy butt told her that they were his, and why should he throw them away?

He said she acted like she wanted to physically fight him; after all, she was a little bigger and taller than he was.

I called Cindy and told her the story. She told me to stay out of it and let Cam handle his own business. I agreed.

So every time he called, I would just listen. I didn't want him to go back and say, "Well, Richard said . . ." in his conversation with her. I didn't want to give him any ammo against me. So I stayed quiet and listened to his moaning.

A few weeks went by and I didn't hear from Cam. I thought maybe he was working things out with Brandy. I called a few times and my calls went unanswered. I didn't know what was going on between them, but I hoped things had gotten better.

Then, at the end of the week, my phone rang. It was Cam. He was breathing heavily and saying, "Man, I'm going to kill this girl."

"Say what? What's going on now, man? I thought you guys were fixing things?"

Boy, was I wrong about that; things had really gotten out of hand. He told me that she had tried to fight him physically, and that he'd discovered some of his things missing from his house when he got home from work. She couldn't let it go after finding the letters and pictures. He said his brand-new fridge was gone. I guess they had gone half on buying that, but this was the first I had heard of it. He said she took some money and merchandise that he was selling. He was so pissed off that he could hardly get the words out to express how he really felt about her now.

Then the shocker came when he said he had to call the police, and she was still trying to fight him in front of them. He said she hit him in front of the police and they didn't do anything. He asked the police, "You see she hit me, officer, so why aren't you doing anything about it?" Cam said the police just smiled and kept holding her. They only told him to take out a restraining order against her, so she couldn't come back to his place.

When I heard all this mess, I was dying of laughter in my head. I thought, *That's exactly what that fool gets for crossing me with Brandy.* I didn't have to do anything because he was getting his and more. I didn't let him know how I was feeling, though; I just listened to him getting all wound up.

I tried to calm him down and told him that everything happened for a reason, so relax. Then he said, "She even threatened me. She said that if she sees me out, I'm going to get mine."

"Wow! Did she really say that, Cam? Do you think she would do that?" I asked him in total shock.

Cam told me he wasn't really worried about her doing anything to him. He said she'd better not touch him or get anybody after him. I just couldn't believe how this had unfolded. I thought he really was going to marry her. I knew that he really cared for her because he had stopped talking to his old girlfriends, and he spoke of marriage without really getting to know her. Even though I had a nasty taste in my mouth about the situation, I believed he would have treated her right. I guess the way he got her was the reason things went sour.

As I was talking to Cam, I got a beep from the other line on my phone. I told Cam to hold on while I switched lines. It was Dominique, and she asked me if I had time to talk, so I agreed.

"Cam, let me call you back. It's my baby momma," I said with a short breath. Then I switched back over to the other line. "What do you want, Dominique?"

"I just want to tell you a few things about your boy, Leon."

"He's not my boy," I said.

"Well, anyway, remember that time you and he went to Toronto?"

"Yeah, I remember."

"Well, he said you had sex with some girls and gave them your number, and they stayed at the hotel with y'all."

"Say what? That's a damn lie," I said.

"Anyway, he would always tell me everywhere y'all went and what y'all were doing, and that's why I slept with him to get you back. I'm so sorry."

Boy, my blood pressure shot up. *That damn Leon is a low-down boy*, I thought.

"Well, that still doesn't give you the right to sleep with a friend," I said angrily.

"I'm just telling you so you know why."

"Bye, Dominique," I said, and hung up the phone while she was still talking.

I clicked back over. Cam was still on the phone waiting to talk some more. I told him that was Dominique trying to make a plea again. We laughed.

Cam started talking about how he would stay single and never let a woman get close to him again. Who was he kidding? That fool loved him some women just like I did, so that idea was a joke.

Chapter Four

Michelle

Cam and I stayed friends, but I treated him like a long-handled spoon. I kept him as far away from my business as possible. Cindy and I started seeing each other more and more. She had two kids and didn't want me to meet them unless we were really in a relationship. I really didn't understand that at first. Eventually I understood that it made sense, so we just stayed friends and would date here and there.

Then one night I was headed over to Jarvis's house and I saw this girl named Michelle, whom I had known of since we were little kids. She lived downstairs from Jarvis.

Jarvis told me that she had a man living with her and that I knew him from playing basketball. He was a coach and his name was Vincent. I told Jarvis I had seen Michelle looking at me as I came up the stairs.

Jarvis said he never tried to talk to her because his girlfriend was living with him, but she was fine. He told me that I should try to talk to her even though she had someone. I told him that he was crazy.

Every time I came over, she would stop me as I was going up, saying little things to tempt me. At first I ignored it, but then I thought, *Hey, men have done it to me, so why not see her on the side?*

One night we exchanged numbers, while Vincent was in the

house cooking dinner for Michelle and her kid. She called me the next morning and we made plans to meet up that Friday. At first we couldn't figure out where to meet, and then I let her talk me into coming to her house. I was nervous as hell. I asked her, "Are you sure that's safe?"

Michelle said, "Yes, it's safe, because he doesn't have a key to the house."

"He doesn't?" I asked. That kind of shocked me.

"If anybody comes, you can go up the back steps to Jarvis's house."

So I fell for what she said and ended up there that Friday morning. I was trying to be slow and gentle, but she wanted to jump right into it. She had never had foreplay before, so that turned me off a bit. Having sex with her wasn't that good at first. I thought it was because we were both worried about someone coming in. We tried again and that was the same. She was boring, and I think she knew I wasn't turned on because I couldn't come.

The next time we got together, she performed oral sex on me. Now *that* was great. So sex got better with her after that. I guess the oral enhanced the feeling.

At first I didn't feel bad that I was sleeping with her, but then Vincent started talking to me more and more. So I told Michelle that I couldn't sleep with her anymore. She started crying and asking me why. I told her that I was starting to feel guilty. I was once on the other side of the coin, so I knew what we were doing was wrong. She didn't seem to care; she just started falling deeper in love with me, and I didn't know what to do.

So for months and months we would sneak around. I hated even looking Vincent's way because I felt so bad. Then Michelle told me the story behind Vincent. "He cheated on me several times and I took him back," she said with teary eyes.

"Oh, so you are just getting him back?" I asked.

She just nodded her head as if to say yes. She said, "He slept with someone I knew. He could've at least slept with someone I didn't know, right?"

"I don't know, Michelle." It was still wrong. "So why did you take him back?"

"Well, we do have a daughter together. I just wanted her to know her father, I guess."

"Well, you should decide to keep him or not, because I hate this sneaking around."

"Yeah, you're right. I will figure out something soon," she said as she laid her head on my chest.

Then one day I received a called from Michelle. She said, "I kicked Vincent out, so now we don't have to sneak around anymore."

I was shocked. "Say what?"

"Yeah, you heard me. Vincent didn't come home all night."

"That's crazy," I said. "So what happened when you told him?"

"He was upset, but I can't take his shit anymore," she said angrily. "He had the nerve to stay out, and then come home the next night all drunk up."

"That's just plain stupid," I said.

"So we don't have to sneak around anymore, Richard," Michelle said, giggling.

Even though Vincent was no longer living with Michelle, the situation still didn't sit well with me. But I continued to see her. I think I would've stopped talking to her, but her oral sex game had me stuck. Eventually I really started liking her. I saw my feelings toward her changing.

One day she told she was moving to another side of town and that she wanted me to stay with her. I told her I had to think about that. I knew her baby's father would be coming by to see his child, and I already didn't feel good about seeing her behind his back.

Every once in a while I would stay with her, and I started interacting with her kids. She kept begging me to stay, over and over again. I really was falling for her, but I didn't want her to know how I was feeling, so I played hard-to-get.

Then I started leaving clothes at her house, and it seemed as if I had moved in, so every once in a while I would take some of my clothing home.

"Are you going to move in here or what? I will give you the key so you can come in whenever you want," Michelle said, looking up into my eyes.

"Well, give me the key and we'll see," I said with a frustrated look on my face. In the back of my mind, I had always thought that she would leave or do me like she had done Vincent, so I was too scared to commit. I knew that one day, I could be in his shoes.

He would always try to get her back; at least, that was what she would tell me. Whenever he called, Michelle would be so rude and mean to him. I just didn't want that to be me someday.

Even though Michelle and I had been seeing each other for a while, Vincent never knew until one day when I didn't know he was coming to get his kid. I popped up and—bam! He looked shocked and hurt, and I felt his pain. His eyes pierced through me like the laser on a Blu-ray. Oh my God, I didn't feel good about that. He held his composure and didn't say much after that.

Michelle was so cold about him that she said, "So what if he saw us?" She said she didn't care if he saw us together. I couldn't believe how cold she was, and that really worried me to death. I felt that man's pain because I have been in his shoes.

After that he would see me and stop speaking, and half the time he wouldn't even look my way. I felt really low. I told Michelle how I felt and all she would say was, "Why do you feel bad? That's what he gets for cheating on me."

I said, "Well, two wrongs don't make a right." She just looked at me like I was crazy.

I stopped talking about it after that day and just starting thinking about what I would do if the same thing happened to me. I started protecting my heart after that.

Then one evening Michelle said, "I have to move because the tenants next door brought roaches into the complex." She told me that she wasn't going to tell Vincent where she was moving. I thought that was mean because he wouldn't be able to see his child, but she said that was his problem. All I could say to myself was, "Wow."

Michelle moved further to the South Side of town. After she moved in, she told me that Vincent's brothers and mother lived at the other end of the street.

I said loudly, "What the fuck?" I was so pissed off at her. I mean, oh my god! How could she be so careless?

She said to me with a straight face, "They don't deal with my child, or Vincent."

I said, "Bullshit." I meant it too, but I eventually took her word for it and moved some of my things into her house.

What a mistake that was, because all of a sudden we started seeing Vincent walking down the street almost every day. She said that he had lost his car, job, and apartment, so now he was staying down the street with his brothers and his mother.

His brothers were older guys, and not once did I see them come down. Sometimes I would pull up and see Vincent sitting on Michelle's step with their child. I felt so out of place. One day when I came there he actually started speaking to me, and all I could think about was how I had done this guy so wrong.

So now I was trying to make up reasons to break up with her, but it seemed as if she loved me so much. I hoped she wouldn't become a stalker or something. How could I break up with this woman? I was stuck and didn't know what the outcome would be. Lord help me!

Several times I got all my clothes from her house and told her I wasn't coming back, but I always went back. She would talk me into coming over and then seduce me with that good oral sex.

Damn! I was whipped and sprung.

Then one day something crazy happened. Michelle went to work and I was off that day, so I stayed at her house. One of her dresser drawers was open, and I saw papers in it. I opened the drawer and saw that there were letters inside. I wasn't usually the snooping type, but I couldn't fight it.

I opened one of the letters, and it was from one of her ex-boyfriends in prison. He was thanking Michelle for writing him and saying he was glad she'd been reaching out to him. He even asked her how his little girl was doing. I guess he was talking about Michelle's daughter, who to my knowledge was Vincent's child.

I was livid and didn't know what to do. This couldn't be right. I read the letter again. Initially I thought the letter was just him writing to her, but no—he was only writing her back.

That didn't sit well with me. I paced the bedroom floor very fast, thinking about how I should keep this to myself and not tell Michelle that I knew. But this was eating me up so badly that I knew I couldn't keep it in.

I started looking in every drawer and found another letter. *So she's been keeping up with this damn convict*, I thought. I hadn't even known this guy existed.

I couldn't wait till she got home. I now had my ammo to leave, and leaving was exactly what I planned to do. I felt so betrayed, but what had I expected? I always knew in the back of my mind that this would happen because of how I had met her.

I tore up the whole room looking for more information, but that was all I could find. I didn't notice anything in the letter saying that she had come to see him while he was locked up. I was definitely trying to find that.

When she got home, all the drawers were open and I was sitting on the bed, pissed.

"What's going on?" she asked.

"What's up with you?" I answered.

"What do you mean? And why are all these papers everywhere?" Suddenly there was a frown on her face.

"Who in the hell is this guy you've been writing to in prison?" I asked loudly.

"What? You've been doing snooping in my stuff?"

"I wasn't snooping. I saw a paper in the drawer, which was cracked a little open."

"You have no right to go through my stuff, Richard," she said defensively.

"Whatever, whatever. Don't be trying to switch this up on me. Who is he?" I said with both eyebrows raised.

Michelle started pacing the room, picking up all her papers, and putting them back in the drawers. Then she put the two letters on top of the dresser and started trying to explain them. "This guy I used to talk to, his name is Winston. He's been locked up for a few years now, but he's sentenced to twenty-five years for murder. He was caught in another man's house with the other man's woman, and the man came home and he shot him."

"You're still keeping in touch with someone like that? What the hell is wrong with you?"

"Well, it's not like he's going to get out. So what's the issue?" she asked.

I started thinking to myself that this woman was out of her damn mind for keeping up with a killer. I asked her, "How did you know where he was in prison?"

"I got the information from his sister while in the grocery store. Winston's sister said he was asking about me. I didn't expect to hear from him once I had written the first letter, but he started writing back," she said with a sad look.

I wasn't buying that sad look, but I kept on listening and asking questions. "What you mean you didn't expect to hear from him? You wrote him first."

"I didn't think it would mean anything since he's in there for twenty-five years. Even though we had broken up, we were still friends before he committed the crimes."

"You're crazy," I said. "Well, this doesn't sit well with me, so I'm taking my stuff and moving out." Michelle started crying and trying to explain more, but I was already collecting my things.

After leaving Michelle's house that night, I felt so good. My mind was now clear because I had needed to get out of that relationship for a long time. I knew that this time I was out for good.

But, as expected, Michelle called me. She started stalking me. Everywhere I went she was turning up, and it really worried me. I saw her parked in back of my house, just sitting in her car for hours.

One day I came outside and my tires were slit. I couldn't blame Michelle for it because I hadn't seen her do it, but I believed it was her.

One morning I had to call the cops just to get her off the premises. It was crazy for a while. After that, she finally disappeared. She might have gotten back with Vincent, or was waiting on the ex-con to get out. I didn't care. That was enough drama for me.

I promised myself that the next time I got involved with a woman, I would make sure she was marriage material. I set out to be single until I was sure I had found the right one.

Part Three

Nathan's Story

Chapter One

Shana and Her Aunt Shay

I'm Nathan. Yes, yes, at age twenty-one I was still living at home with my momma because it was cheaper. Women laughed at me and so did my friends. I didn't care because I was saving money and having a great time in life. I remember that sunny morning in early July when I got up and the birds were chirping under a pretty blue sky. I came out of the house carrying a radio with an extension cord on it and sat on the porch. I played the oldies-but-goodies.

As I was listening to the song "Back Down Memory Lane," a big U-Haul truck came down the street, with a few cars following close behind. Some people jumped out of the truck. A guy and two women got out and went straight to the door of an empty house down the street.

I peeped down the street to see who our new neighbors were. One was nicely curvy and the other was very thick, but they both looked sexy from where I was sitting.

After hours and hours of moving their stuff into the house, the two women came walking past my mother's house. The nicely curved one was light-skinned with greenish-hazel eyes. She stopped and introduced herself. "Hello, we are your new neighbors down the street. My name is Shana and this is my aunt Shay," she said with a lot of energy. We all began shaking hands and smiling at one another. "Hi, I'm Shay," her aunt said.

"Hi, I'm Nathan," I said. "How are you guys doing?"

"We are so tired from moving all day," Shay said, just as excited and full of life as Shana.

Shana and Shay went to the store. On their way back, they stopped in front of the house and started dancing to Marvin Gaye's "Sexual Healing." Everybody started laughing and just enjoyed the moment. Shana and Shay had two big bags of alcoholic drinks and chips. They said, "After all that moving, we are ready to party." When the song changed they invited me to come down and drink with them anytime I liked.

I quickly agreed. "I will be down there as soon as I get dressed."

"Don't take too long, because all the drinks will be gone. My family drinks like fish," Shay said, laughing.

"For real, she isn't lying," Shana said.

As they went down the street, I went in the house to get all dressed up. Even though they were both good-looking, Shay was more my type; she had some pretty catlike eyes. I thought about her as I was getting dressed. Both women seemed interested in me, though, so I just went with the flow. After getting dressed I put my favorite cologne on, hit the door, and headed down the street. When I got to the house, the music was loud and everyone was on the porch drinking.

Shana went and got me a glass and poured me a drink. Then she sat near me and we started talking.

"How long have you lived on this street, Nathan?" Shana asked.

"Too long."

"Who do you live with down there?" Shay asked, sitting on the porch railing.

I laughed and said, "I live there with my mom."

"Why are you saying it like that?"

"People start laughing when I tell them that I stay home with my momma, especially my friends."

"They are just jealous because they probably can't stay with their momma," Shay said with a serious look.

"I know that's right," Shana said.

They both were nice women, and they both seemed interested in me. Shana was a little more aggressive, and I really liked that. Our vibe was strong. When Shay got up and went into the house, Shana and I began to get a little more personal. She asked me if I had anyone in my life and I asked her the same. Shana said that she and her husband had broken up and that she was waiting on their divorce to be final.

"Girl, how old are you? You seem too young to be married and divorced already," I said.

Shana said she had gotten married at eighteen, and she was now twenty-five. She looked a year or so younger, but she was older than I was. I couldn't believe she had been married already.

"Why did you and your husband separate?" I asked.

"He was too controlling, and I just found out that he's already engaged and our divorce isn't even final yet. Isn't that crazy, Nathan?" she asked.

After that day Shana and I became closer. I would go down to her house and get drunk, which made me feel relaxed. Sometimes I even used to stay the night.

I can remember the night we first made love. It was after we had been drinking. The mood was right. We had Luther Vandross on and the candles lit. I began kissing her and caressing her very gently.

Then all I heard was heavy breathing and soft screams of joy. It was sweet music to my ears. The next morning when we woke up, Shay said, "Can you guys be any quieter up there?"

Shana and I looked at each other and laughed, and so did Shay. Then, as Shana turned around, Shay winked at me as if to say she liked what she had heard between her niece and me. I just laughed and got in the shower. I put my clothes on and went down the street back to my mom's house.

I was having so much fun with Shana; I didn't want this good time to end. She was down to earth, exciting, and very sexy with those catlike eyes. But I didn't know what to think about the way Shay would look at me when I came over. She would even flirt with me, but I never said anything to Shana about it. Shay used to flirt with me in front of Shana, so there wasn't a reason to say anything anyway.

One day some new guys moved around the corner, and they walked by Shana's house.

"Hi, I'm Herald," a dark-skinned guy said.

His friend wasn't much of a talker, but he would always stare at everybody. He was sort of rough looking, and it seemed as if he was living in the street life. I really didn't like him at all, and Herald didn't seem all that cool either.

I used to leave the house and come back to Shana's house, and Herald would be sitting on the steps. I didn't really think anything of it because everybody knew that Shana and Shay's house was now the neighborhood party spot.

But then it got to the point where Herald was there every day, and sometimes he acted like he didn't want to go home. I never said anything to Shana because it was her house.

One night, I told her, "I'm staying home down at Mom's tonight."

"Okay. Will you be back tomorrow?"

"Yeah, I will be back to stay the night tomorrow," I said.

That next morning I woke up at around six in the morning, peeped out the door, and looked down the street. I saw Herald coming out of Shana's house. I saw Shana's arm closing the door. I was so damned pissed off that I didn't know what to say. We hadn't made our relationship official, but I thought we were getting somewhere, especially since she was still waiting for her divorce to be finalized.

After that I didn't say anything to Shana about seeing Herald come out of her house that morning. I just began flirting with Shay behind Shana's back.

One day Shay said to me with a pained look on her face, "You know my niece and Herald have been seeing each other when you're not here, right?"

"I kind of figured that out when I saw him coming out of the house one morning."

"You didn't say anything?"

"Nope, I didn't and I'm not going to."

"Well, you're better than me because I would have said something to both of them."

"I really like Shana, but we never made it official so I can't really get too upset."

"Yeah, but right is right, and that shit isn't right," Shay said.

I couldn't believe that Shana's own aunt was telling on her like this. I asked Shay, "So why are you telling on your niece?"

"Well, that's my niece and I love her, but I heard she slept with my ex behind my back."

"Wow, are you serious?" I asked. I was shocked to hear that news.

Then I heard Shana say from the other room, "Nathan, I'm going to the store."

"Okay, I will be right here when you get back!" I yelled.

Once Shana had left for the store, Shay grabbed my hand and took me to the basement. She took me way in the back of the basement, pulled down her skirt, and told me to have sex with her. I was shocked.

"What?" I asked with a crazy look on my face. "Are you serious?"

She said, "Yes. Put it in me. I hear how you've been rocking my niece's world up there sometimes."

She began rubbing on my manhood, and next thing I knew, I was inside her going to work. She was trying to be quiet and so was I, but I knew we didn't have much time. I couldn't let Shana hear us or see us. So we made it a quickie—but a good quickie. I couldn't believe it had happened so fast.

"Don't say anything," Shay said.

"I won't, and you'd better not either," I replied.

As soon as we got our clothes on and went back upstairs, Shana came through the door. We had finished right in the nick of time. Shay went her way and I went my way, and it was like nothing had ever happened.

After that day I stopped going down to Shana's house as much to see her. Every time she would leave, Shay would pull me to the basement and we would do our thing, and that would be it.

I didn't have feelings for Shay like I did for Shana, so it started to get boring. Finally I stopped going down there altogether. I would sit on my mom's porch, just chilling. Shay and Shana would ask me if I was coming down, but I would make up an excuse not to go there.

Then I started seeing Shana and Herald walk by the house. They must have really gotten into each other because they would hold hands while walking by me. I didn't let it bother me. I would just keep listening to my music. I wasn't going to let this mess get me all jacked up.

One night Shay came down to my mom's house and asked me to have sex with her in back of the house.

"Come on, girl, with your horny self," I said quietly because everyone was asleep.

"Okay, okay. I'm glad I wore this skirt with no panties," Shay said quietly with a big smile on her face. I pulled the skirt up and began stroking her fast and hard. She was moaning so loudly that I had to keep going and stopping. Her body started trembling and she climaxed so hard. I thought, *Damn, it must be good to her*. After we finished, I pulled my pants up and we said our good-byes.

I went in the house and cleaned up, and Shay walked down the street carefully. She looked sort of bowlegged and staggering. I started smiling. *I must have done a good job on her*, I thought.

Shay just couldn't get enough of me; she kept coming back for more. Then one day I heard that Herald and Shana had stopped talking for some reason. Shana came down the street and started talking to me while I was on the steps.

"How are you doing, Nathan?"

"I'm good, and yourself?"

"I guess you heard Herald and I aren't talking anymore?"

"Yeah, I heard. Well, what happened?" I asked with my head down.

"It's a long story, but are you mad at me because Herald and I started talking?"

"I must admit I was at first, but now I'm okay."

"Well, Nathan, I still care for you, Plus we are like family, so you can start coming back down to see me sometimes," she said with a serious look. I looked at her like she was crazy. She didn't realize it, though.

So after that I started going back down to Shana's house, but we weren't trying to be like we were before. We were good friends now—friends with benefits, I guess. Shay seemed to love the fact that I was hanging out with them again. She would get herself some every chance she could.

Then on Shana's birthday, everyone got together for a party. Everyone was getting drunk and falling out everywhere, and I mean *everywhere*—on the couch, the floor.

A bunch of people went home. I was so drunk that Shana and Shay took me upstairs in the bedroom and laid me on the floor. They were both pretty drunk, too. We all crashed on the floor and went to sleep.

I woke up an hour later because I heard someone snoring. I looked to my left and saw that it was Shay, who was knocked out. I nudged Shana, who woke up and pulled me on top of her while Shay was knocked out. We had sex for a while, and then Shana passed out. I turned and nudged Shay.

Then I got her from the side while I kept looking to make sure

Shana didn't wake up. Then after that I was out. All of us were.

They were so drunk that the next day they didn't remember what had happened. It was a wonderful night, and after that we all remained friends.

Chapter Two

Mary and Floyd

After I messed around with Shay and Shana, my mom decided to move off the street. I didn't see them that much after that, but when I did we showed love for one another.

I started hanging out at my friend Jarvis's house over on the South Side. He had met this girl named Renee at the mall and said that she had some pretty friends. So every time I would go to his house, they would look at me as if they were competing over who would get me first. Then Jarvis told me that I should talk to Mary, who had money because her dad was a black pilot.

"For real, man? Are you serious?" I asked him.

"Yeah, they live out in the suburbs and have a really large house. I've been out there, and they have a pool and everything," he said, smiling. He told me that Mary had asked about me a few times. She was brown-skinned, very petite but with curves and very pretty light brown eyes. She acted too shy for me, though, so I was undecided as to whether or not I should talk to her.

Then one day at a Super Bowl party at Jarvis's house, she spoke to me in a flirtatious way. I was shocked but answered with something cute, and we smiled. So throughout the evening we kept talking and flirting with each other. Then I finally asked her for her phone number, but I eased it in very slick. "Do you want to exchange numbers? I think we need to talk about some things?"

She laughed and said, "Oh, really? So what do we need to talk about, Nathan? The birds and the bees?" That made me laugh really hard.

The next day Jarvis called me, asking all these nosy questions. "So what do think about Mary? I told you she was fine as hell, didn't I? So when are you guys going out? Do you like her?" Jarvis just kept the questions rolling.

"Yeah, I think she's sexy and very intelligent, and I'm going to take her out sometime soon. Any more questions, Detective?" I said jokingly.

"Well, man, just let me know how things go with the both of you."

"I will, Detective Nosy Guy. I will, I will, I will," I said. Jarvis laughed.

A few hours later the phone rang, and it was Mary. "Hello there. How are you doing today?" she asked.

"Hi. I'm doing well. Thank you for asking." We began talking about many things, from family to how our lives were going. It seemed as if we had a lot in common, like goals, dreams, and the fact we both loved our families.

"Why don't you have anyone special in your life, Nathan?"

"Well, I was waiting on you," I said, as if I was a smooth operator.

"Yeah, right," Mary said, giggling. "That was a good one. So when was the last time you were in a relationship?"

I hesitated for a moment before answering the question because I didn't want her to think that I jumped from relationship to relationship. I let her know that I was sort of in a relationship, but Shana and I hadn't made it official. Mary understood where I was coming from because she said she had gone through the same thing.

"Well, what's your ex-friend's name? Where is he now?" I asked curiously.

"Well, he's still around but we don't have anything to do with each other. He was at the Super Bowl party, Jarvis's cousin Floyd," she said in a low voice."

"What?" I said. "Who? Oh no, you have to be playing," I said seriously. That threw me for a loop. Floyd was Jarvis's cousin and sort of a friend to me. I couldn't understand why Jarvis hadn't told me. Why hook me up with someone he knew had dated my friend?

"Is that a problem?" Mary asked.

I didn't want to be rude so I said, "No problem, no problem." In the back of my mind I knew it was a problem. Now I felt like I had a dilemma. What should I do now?

After Mary and I got off the phone, I called Jarvis. "Why didn't you tell me she dated your cousin Floyd, man?"

"Man, he didn't know how to treat her, and they didn't talk that long. He never made it official," Jarvis said.

"I think you still should have told me, man. I mean, damn."

"You're right. So what are you going to do? Floyd would have done it to you."

After talking to Jarvis I got off the phone, I started thinking. I knew that Floyd would be a little upset when he found out. I didn't care what Jarvis had just said on the phone. Deep down inside I knew it wasn't right, and I couldn't understand why he and Mary couldn't see that.

One day I saw Floyd when I was out, and I approached him about Mary. "Hey, Floyd, what's up, man?"

"Nothing much, Nathan. What's up with you?"

"Nothing much, but I needed to ask you a question," I said.

"Go ahead and ask," Floyd said in a light voice.

"What's up with you and Mary? Are you still interested in her?" I asked.

He said, with a shocked look on his face, "Oh, we used to talk, but it wasn't anything serious."

"Are you sure, man?" I asked. "We've been talking, and I just found out you and she had been talking. I didn't know that at first. Do you have a problem with her talking to me now?"

"No, go ahead, man. Do your thing." He didn't look convincing.

He sounded as if he didn't care, but his facial expressions said something else. He assured me that there wasn't anything between him and Mary. So I took his word for it because she had said that they never made it official.

So after the conversation with Floyd, Mary and I began dating. I used to feel so uncomfortable when we all were around each other. Every time I came over Jarvis's house, Floyd would be there too. I would be hugging Mary or holding her hand, and when I glanced at Floyd, he would be frowning. I tried to not pay him any attention. If he had said he didn't want me to talk to her because he really cared about her, I probably wouldn't have. He told me it was okay, but now I wasn't so sure. Mary would act as if he wasn't even in the room with us. They wouldn't speak to or look at each other when I was around.

So one day I asked Mary, "Why don't you and Floyd speak anymore?"

"We do speak sometimes, Nathan."

"When? When I'm around I never see you guys speak."

"Well, I respect you, so we don't chat with each other."

"You guys don't have to act like enemies while I'm around either," I said.

Mary didn't reply to that statement, so I just left it alone and didn't ask any more questions. It just seemed odd to me.

After that talk with Mary, she came over to my aunt's house to meet me there. My aunt had gone out of town, so I was watching her house for her.

We began kissing, hugging, and caressing each other. The next minute we were making love all over the house. I had her legs on my shoulders. I stood up and walked around the house with her. She was breathing so heavily, and her eyes looked as if she had never felt this way before.

After about an hour and a half, we sat on the side of the bed and began talking. Her body was trembling uncontrollably, and we both looked at each other and laughed. Then she got up to use the bathroom and stumbled a little. The wall had to keep her from falling.

I was smiling my behind off because she looked as if she had just won the lottery.

Mary came back in the room mumbling something. At first I couldn't make out what she was saying. Then I heard her say, "Wow, no one has ever made me feel that way before while making love. You made me have multiple orgasms, and that has never happened."

"Never ever? Are you for real, Mary?"

"I swear, I am not lying—when I had sex with Floyd it was nothing like what we just did. It happened so fast that I can't even remember how it felt," she said with a straight face.

"Damn, so it was that good?" I asked with a smile on my face. It made me feel so good to know that I had satisfied her like that. Sex was good with Mary, so I knew for sure that we would do it again.

Then she turned to me and said, "Another thing is that his penis isn't as big as yours, and you know how to work it really well. I was, like, oh my God, in heaven."

"Wow. Well, thank you. It's a must that I please my lady. With me you will always be pleased, Mary."

After that talk, we showered and got dressed. Mary kissed me, and then we went our separate ways. I thought to myself, *I really like this girl.* It felt so good to be with her that I didn't want our time together to end.

Mary called me late one night and told me that Floyd called her. I was shocked. "What did he say?' I asked.

"Not much—he just asked me how I was doing and asked me if I really liked you."

"So what did you tell him?"

"I told him that, yes, I do and that he needs to stop calling me," she said.

"So how did he react to that when you told him?"

"He said he was just checking on me because he still cares about me. I told him that I was good and that we were doing well, so no need to worry."

I couldn't believe this clown had called Mary and asked her these questions. I wondered what else he had said to her, because to me it seemed as if she was holding back information.

After that call my guard went way up. I knew that I couldn't trust Floyd. Why would he call Mary when he knew we were talking? Why would he ask her those questions about her and me? I couldn't make heads or tails of it. I knew that I had to ask him about it when I saw him.

I got his number from Jarvis and called several times, but my calls went unanswered. I went looking for him at his regular hang-out spots and still couldn't find him.

Time went by, and Mary and I were really getting into each other. Our feelings were getting stronger, until one day somebody from my past decided to stop over and surprise me. I didn't even know that she was going to stop by. That day changed everything.

I was sitting on the steps of my mother's house when a shiny black Honda pulled up. The rims were clean and the tires were low. It even had a sunroof, which was open. It was a bad ride, I tell you.

It was my high school sweetheart, Tonya. I hadn't seen her in a few years.

She was looking so good. She had a dark chocolate complexion and great legs. She was thick with a small waist and 38D breasts. She smiled and got out of the car, smelling so good that I could smell her from the house to the car.

"Nathan, who is that?" my mom asked.

"Do you remember Tonya, my high school girlfriend?"

"Oh, you mean the girl you were all in love with whose parents had a lot of money."

"Yes, that's her. Now shhh, shhhhh, she's coming over here," I said.

Tonya came toward the steps where I was sitting. She smiled and gave me a really big hug. My mom spoke to Tonya, and then I escorted her into the house so we could chat in privacy.

"What's up, Nathan? How have you been doing?"

"I've been good, T. How have you been doing?" I asked with a grin on my face. "How did you know where I lived?"

"I was riding by and I saw you sitting out here. At first I wasn't sure, but then I looked again. I had to turn around and talk to my high school sweetheart."

I laughed and said, "So you noticed me just driving by?"

"Yes, I sure did."

Tonya stayed for hours talking about old times. At one point when we were laughing, Tonya leaned over to give me a hug and a kiss on the cheek, which was unexpected. I looked up and saw that Mary was pulling up.

I wasn't expecting her, so I was shocked. She had a hurt look on her face and just took off. I felt so bad that I hollered out to her, but she was flying. I felt like crap.

Tonya looked me and said, "Who was that? I hope I didn't get you in any trouble."

"It's this girl I'm talking to named Mary. It's cool. I will explain to her later."

"Okay, Nathan. Well, it was good to see you."

"It's good to see you, too. Leave a number so we can stay in touch," I said.

Tonya gave me her number, and then left. I tried calling Mary to explain, but there was no answer. I couldn't connect with her at all.

Days turned into weeks, and weeks turned into months. I couldn't believe Mary; she wouldn't even give me a chance to explain. Everything was innocent with Tonya; I hadn't even known that she was coming that day.

Then one day I went by Jarvis's house and saw Mary's car outside. I went in and saw Floyd and Mary hugged up and kissing in the corner. I immediately blew my top. Floyd and I started arguing, and the boys had to hold us apart.

"This what you do Mary? You didn't even give me a chance to explain."

"You were cheating on me," she said with tears and drool falling down her lips.

I was so hurt after that situation. I couldn't believe that she would go back to Floyd, especially given how she had talked about his performance in bed.

I knew I had to get his ass back, so one day while at the market I saw Mena, his baby momma. I started telling her all the dirt I had on Floyd. She got so pissed.

Mena invited me over later that evening. I guess she wanted more information. I took some drinks and we ordered food. She said that her and Floyd's daughter was at her mother's house for the weekend, so we were all alone.

Yeah, all that pillow talking he was doing? Yeah, that's right—I was telling. I knew that it was against the man code, but I began spilling the beans. After we had finished talking, she put in a movie and dimmed the lights. Those drinks had us both feeling a certain type of way.

One thing led to another, and soon we was in her bed going at it. We were making such passionate love. I wondered how in the hell Floyd had let this one go.

After we finished, she was shaking and trembling, and the same thing came out of her mouth that had come out of Mary's mouth after we made love for the first time. She told me that Floyd wasn't as good as I was in bed and that his equipment was way smaller. I just laughed. As she got up to go to the bathroom, she was still having an orgasm. We talked some more, and then I showered. After that we hugged and I went home.

I was happy as hell, because I felt like I had gotten Floyd back for what he did. He knew Mary was vulnerable and he used that against me. The only problem was that I wished he knew I had been with his baby momma.

Chapter Three

Nikki Slept With My Cousin Hank

Then I met this sexy girl named Nikki who had an hourglass figure, a beautiful smile, and pretty brown eyes that shone when the sun hit them. I met her through my cousin Tracey. Nikki had been hanging over my cousin's house for a while. She would always look at me and smile, but I didn't know what to think of it. I had just gotten out my last relationship with Mary, so I didn't know if I should pursue another relationship so fast off the hills.

One day Tracey walked up to me and said, "Nikki likes you, cuz. I think she wants some of that thang-thang." She giggled. "Go ahead and give it to her, cuz."

I laughed and said, "I'll think about it."

Then, as my cousin walked away laughing, Nikki walked up to me and said, "Did Tracey tell you that I like you and want to talk to you?"

"Yes, she did, but I thought she was just playing."

"No, I told her, 'Damn, your cousin Nathan is fine, girl. I wish I could make him mine.'"

"What did she say when you said that?"

"Well I'm over here talking to you, right? She said go ahead because both of us are grown."

"So you're not talking to anyone and don't have a man?" I asked.

She asked, "No, do you?"

I said, "Hell no, I don't have a man." We both just started laughing.

One thing about Nikki was that she had a great sense of humor, and she was full of fire. I really liked that about her. We exchanged numbers and kept in touch a lot after that day. The things she would say used to crack me up. We would be crying with laughter on the phone. We would stay up all night talking about the people we knew and the crazy stuff they did.

Every day after I got off work, I would go by Tracey's house to chill out. Nikki started hanging over there a lot, and eventually she started living with my cousin and paying half the expenses.

So this was my new hangout spot, and I was loving being around Nikki. We spent so much time together that it was like we were best friends. I really enjoyed being with her. She helped me to forget all about Mary and Floyd.

Then one day Jarvis called me and told me that Mary and Floyd had broken up. He said, "She only got back with my cuz because she was hurt by you."

I explained to Jarvis what really had happened, and all he could say was, "Wow. So nothing happened with you and the girl she saw you with?"

"Nope, not at all. You remember I told you about Tonya from school? Well, she just popped up and Mary saw her hug me and kiss me on the cheek."

"Wow, now that's crazy."

"Yes, it is, but that's okay because I met this girl named Nikki, and she is nice and sexy."

"You in love again, Nathan?"

"Shut up, man," I said, and we both laughed.

After that conversation with Jarvis, Nikki called me and asked me if I wanted to go out to dinner. I said yes. So after work that Friday, I got out of my work clothes, got dressed, and headed over to pick Nikki up.

When I got to my cousin's house, Nikki was standing out front with her hair done. It was long, straight, and jet black. She had a nicely fit dress on that showed all her curves. When she got in the car, all I smelled was a fresh, sweet scent. Oh my goodness, she looked and smelled good. Now that was my kind of woman. I complimented her as she got in the car, and she did the same to me. I couldn't wait to enjoy her that evening.

We went to a nice seafood restaurant that had a very elegant atmosphere. It was a very classy place. We ordered wine once we got to our table, and then we began staring at each other and smiling. Nikki was really working me, because she was all I could think about.

"How are you feeling tonight, Nikki?" I asked smoothly.

"I'm doing fine, and yourself, Mr. Handsome?" she asked jokingly.

"Everything is good. Now let's order some food because I am hungry."

"Yes, sir, and so am I—I mean, hungry for you and the food," she said, flirting a little.

Dinner was very nice; we really enjoyed each other's company. After I paid the bill, we decided to find a hotel, so we could have a little privacy. We finished the night off just right, with a nightcap.

After the nightcap—which was very beautiful, I might add—Nikki and I became even closer than before. We would take late-night walks and surprise each other with gifts. She made me forget all my fears about being in a relationship. I knew we had something special.

One day Nikki asked me, "Have you ever thought about being married?"

"Yes, I have thought about it, and I'm not scared of getting married," I said. "What about you? How do you feel about marriage?"

"I would love to be somebody's wife one day."

"Somebody's?" I asked with a frown on my face.

"Well, yours, of course," she said, and we both laughed.

"You know what I mean, Nathan."

"I know, just messing with you."

"Well, we will see what the future holds, won't we?"

I think Nikki was trying to tell me something when she asked those marriage questions. I was feeling her too, but I knew marriage would be far in the future.

Nikki hugged me tight. The mood was right and the moon was out, so we stood there looking at the sky and the stars with dreams of happily ever after. It was a very nice night.

After that lovely night it seemed as if everything was right for Nikki and me. Then one day Tracey told me that our cousin Hank from South Carolina was coming up here and that he would be staying with her when he came. I didn't think anything of it; I loved Hank and his Southern ways.

Hank came up here from South Carolina midsummer, and it was good to see him. We hadn't seen each other since the last family reunion, which had been about seven years ago. We were cool. I let Hank hang out with me until he eventually met some friends of his own.

Hank was about six foot one, dark-skinned, and very charming. He had waves in his hair, and I knew that women up north would just love him with that Southern drawl.

I never thought anything of him staying with Tracey and Nikki because he was family and she was my girl. It never dawned on me that he might look at my woman in that way.

After he had been up here for a few months, we were having lots of fun so I started telling him some of my secrets. I thought I could trust him.

Then one day I came over to Tracey's house and saw Hank and Nikki talking alone outside. But I still didn't pay it any mind because we all were family.

Then Nikki started acting funny toward me. It seemed as if she was trying to say smart stuff to me to make me argue with her. I didn't understand it because we had been doing so well.

Then one day as I was coming home from work, I saw Hank and Nikki walking home from the store together. At that point I wasn't feeling good about the situation. I was jealous, but didn't say anything. I realized that while I was working all day, they had lots of time to be alone together.

As I got out of the car, Nikki just ignored me and went in the house to put away whatever she had brought from the store. Hank just looked at me with an evil grin. I thought that the grin wasn't very nice, but I stayed quiet.

That day as I sat out there with my cousin, Nikki didn't say one word to me. I wondered what could have done wrong. Everything had been so good. Because Nikki wasn't speaking to me, I said good-bye to everyone and went home with an empty feeling inside.

I couldn't make heads or tails of what was going on until Tracey called me later that night. As I picked up the phone, Tracey whispered, "I think Nikki and cousin Hank are sleeping with each other."

"Say what?"

"Yeah, I caught him coming out of her room at about five on Tuesday morning. He didn't see me, but I heard them talking. Then it got really quiet."

"That's messed up." I was so damn hurt and angry at the same time. How could they do this to me?

After hearing that bad news, I figured I would act as if I didn't know they were messing around behind my back. So one day Nikki brought her friend over Tracey's house. It was someone she had known since they were kids. Her name was Rhonda.

Rhonda was an attractive plus-size woman—nice smile, pretty eyes, and very intelligent. She was about five foot nine with a very big butt that looked like you could set a glass on it. We called it "table booty." It was well proportioned, though.

I saw her staring at me, but being very slick about it. All I could do was smile. Nikki had no idea what was going on. I saw Hank's trifling ass staring at Rhonda like he was going to get that, but I quickly put a monkey wrench in his game. I told Rhonda that he was broke and didn't have a job. She started cracking up.

Then Tracey asked me to go to the liquor store to get some drinks. I asked loudly, "Does anybody need to go to the store?"

Rhonda said, "Yeah, I want something, so is it all right that I go with you?"

"Sure you can. Come on," I said. As I headed to the car, I started smiling. I knew it was time to get to work. Nikki thought she was going to play me for a fool, but I had plans to get her back.

As soon as Rhonda got in the car, I went to work on her. I started telling her about Hank and Nikki and what they were doing behind my back. She was very shocked and a little upset because she had known Nikki since they were kids. She couldn't believe that Nikki would do something like that. She started feeling bad for me. She gave me a hug in the car and said everything would be all right.

When I heard that, a big smile came to my face. So we got the drinks and just rode around for a while talking. We even opened up the drinks that we had bought and began drinking.

"I like you, Nathan. You're a cool guy," she said, a little tipsy.

"I like you, too. I think we should hurry up and get back before they start thinking things," I said with a smile.

"So what? Who cares?"

"Yeah, who cares? I sure don't."

I started staring at those juicy thighs Rhonda had and licking my lips. They were starting to look *mmmmmmmm* good. As I looked back up, Rhonda caught me. Our eyes met and we started laughing.

"You want some of this, don't you?" Rhonda teased.

"I sure do, and you want to give me some too, don't you?"

"Maybe I do, but where can we go?" she asked with a big, pretty smile on her face. "We're going to have to make this fast because we have to get back to Tracey's house."

I could see the lust in her eyes. Her eyes had that hazy look, like she was ready. I shocked about how fast this had come about. I was also ready to get Nikki back by sleeping with her friend because she had been sleeping with Hank behind my back.

So we rode by the park. I parked the car and we both started looking at each other. Then we just smiled.

"Since I have this skirt on, all I have to do is pull it up, because I don't wear panties," Rhonda said.

"No panties? Are you kidding me?" I said excitedly.

"None, so let's get out and make this happen."

We got out and started walking in the park. It was very dark, but we didn't care. I guess you could say that the alcohol was really working in overdrive. We both were so horny that we didn't care where it was going to happen. We found a spot way at the back of the park and stopped. All of a sudden we started kissing, and it was the most passionate kiss I had ever had. We just couldn't stop. I swear, it had to be about twenty minutes before we stopped.

She was a great kisser—it was the best kiss I had ever had in my life. I was like, *Wow!* We were still kissing as I turned her around and lifted up her skirt. I finally got her turned around.

"Do you have protection?" she turned around and asked.

I had my hand in my pocket, already pulling out my protection. "I sure do, so you don't have to worry," I said, anxious to put it in.

We started going at it, and all I could hear was Rhonda moaning and groaning. We had to cut it short, though, because we were in the park and car lights kept popping up.

After we finished, we got back in the car and started talking about that kiss. It was so passionate that it had both of our minds blown away. It made the sex feel so much better.

Then my phone rang. It was Tracey asking me where we were with the drinks. "You've been gone a good while with Rhonda." She giggled.

I think she had an idea of what we were doing, or at least it seemed that way. I just laughed a little and reassured her that we were coming. "We are on our way now, so chill out, Tracey," I said playfully.

"Yeah, okay. See you when you get here, playa."

When we finally made it back, I didn't even look Nikki's way. Hank sat there with a smirk on his face. We began pouring drinks. Music was playing, and then we started playing Spades. We stayed up till the wee hours of the morning. I took Rhonda home that morning, and we exchanged numbers as she got out of the car.

After that night I stopped going to Tracey's house as much. One day Tracey called me and told me that Nikki had moved out. That was music to my ears.

I guess my cousin Hank couldn't handle the city life; he moved back down to South Carolina. Even though he was family, he wasn't right, so I was glad to hear that he had left.

Chapter Four

Frank and Lucy

After all that mess with Nikki, I set out to stay single for a while. Rhonda and I stayed in touch, and every now and then we would see each other, but it wasn't anything too serious.

One day while sitting on the steps in front of my mother's house, I decided to walk down to the corner store. When I went in the store I saw this sexy Latina girl. She walked to the back of the store where the coolers were to get something to drink. I went in to buy something sweet. She was very pretty. She was about five foot nine with beautiful greenish-brown eyes, long hair, and a nice shape. Our eyes locked as we came to register, and we both smiled.

"I see you came to get some sweets, huh? A sweet tooth maybe?" she asked.

"Yes, I sure did. I think I've been fiening," I said and laughed.

"I hear you. I had to come get my soda, so I guess we are both fiening for something," she giggled.

"We should be fiening for each other," I said with a flirtatious look.

"I guess you're right," she laughed. "Hi, my name is Lucy."

"Hi, I'm Nathan. Do you live around here, and are you single?"

"Sort of. My son's father is locked up in jail."

"Oh, okay. Well, is it all right if we exchange numbers and talk later?"

"Yes, sure we can. By the way, I live four blocks away on Kern Street," Lucy said.

"Okay, we live right around the corner from each other, because I stay down the street," I said with a grin.

As soon as I got home from the store, Lucy called me. I sat out back on my mother's steps and started eating my sweets as I started a conversation with her. "Have you ever talked to a Latina girl before?" she asked.

"No, can't say that I have, but I always thought Latina girls were hot."

"Well, technically, I'm mixed. My dad is African American and my mom is from Puerto Rico, but I speak fluent Spanish because my mom used to teach me. She would speak to me in Spanish when I was little and explain to me what the words meant."

"Well, that's good. Your dad must have been light-skinned," I said. "I wouldn't have been able to tell that you were mixed if you hadn't said anything."

"Yes, my dad was light-skinned," she said.

Lucy and I started talking about a little of everything once the ice had been broken. She even told me about her little son. I asked about her son's father and she said his name was Frank. He had gotten locked up for violating probation. I guessed that he had been locked up for a while because she said she had been alone for almost two years. She didn't know exactly when he was getting out. She assured me that she wasn't going to get back with him whenever he did get out.

I wasn't too sure about that, but I just listened as she carried on about her life. After that we would talk on the phone every day, and even went out on dates.

Lucy was a breath of fresh air, and I really enjoyed her company. Sometimes she would speak in Spanish and try to teach me the language, but I would mess up the words, and then we would laugh.

I started staying over her house. She would always have me come over when her son was asleep, because she didn't want him to see another man in the house. I respected her wishes, so late-night rendezvous were a regular thing. Lucy would cook me some Spanish dishes. She was a very good cook. She said that her grandmother had taught her how to cook those good old rice and beans and pulled pork entrees.

That food was beginning to fatten me up, but I enjoyed her cooking. Sometimes when I came over, Lucy would be upset because Frank would call her from jail and say mean things to her.

"I told him that we can't be together when he gets out, and he started yelling and screaming at me," she said sadly.

"Is he crazy or something?" I asked her.

"He said I'd better not have another man around his son."

"Wow, now that is crazy. So what are you going to do?"

"If he gets out and starts messing with me, I'm going to call the cops and put his ass back in jail," she said.

I thought to myself, *What in the hell I have gotten myself into now?* I was no coward, so I knew someday Frank and I would cross paths.

Then there would be other days when Lucy was so happy. We would go for walks. One day we were near my mother's house, so I decided to introduce her to my mom.

As we were walking up, we saw Mom sitting the steps. I said with a smile on my face, "Mom, this Lucy. Lucy, this is my mother."

"Hi, Lucy. You're so pretty."

"Thank you," Lucy said, blushing.

"Take good care of this one," my mom said to me as she walked in the house. "Nice to meet you, Lucy," she said as reached the top of the stairs.

"I like your mom. She is so sweet and looks young."

"Thank you. I think she likes you."

We started walking back around the corner to Lucy's house, holding hands. It felt so good to be with someone with whom I had a lot in common, and the chemistry was in deniable. I let her know exactly how I felt about her, and also told her what I had been through in past relationships. I wasn't going to just jump into relationships anymore, and she said she understood.

The great thing that Lucy and I had was communication. She loved to talk and I loved to listen. I understood her and she understood me, which was very rare.

Deep down this relationship was making me scared, because I was really falling for her. It seemed like she was feeling the same because she always gave me her full attention when I talked. Sometimes when I talked about something that made me sad, she would hug me and kiss me, so I knew she was on the same page as I was. I hoped nothing would interfere with the relationship we were building.

Then one day out of nowhere, Lucy called me and told me that Frank was getting out of jail. He had told her that he was coming by when he got out. Someone, maybe one of the neighbors or one of his friends riding by, had told him that she was seeing a guy and had him around his son.

"He doesn't know that it's me, though?" I asked her.

"I told think so. I mean, how could he?"

"If he does come, just call the cops like you said you would, Lucy."

"I will call them on his crazy ass."

All kind of things started racing through my head. My palms got sweaty, and I felt nervous because I didn't want him to hurt her. After that conversation I didn't hear from her for days. I called her and left messages. I was beginning to get very worried. I didn't want to show up at her house, because I knew Frank was getting out soon. So now I was playing the waiting game. I was trying to see if she would contact me first, but nothing.

One evening while I was on my way to Mom's house, I saw a guy pacing back and forth in front of the house. He didn't look familiar.

He looked like a bodybuilder. He was about six feet tall with a brown-skinned complexion. He was breathing heavily. As soon as I was about to pull out my key and open up door, he said in a deep voice, "Do you know anybody named Nathan?"

"Yeah, why? Who are you?" I said with my chest out.

"I'm Frank, and I heard you've been talking to my girl. I can't have you coming around my son or the house again," he said forcefully.

I asked him loud and clear, "Do you know me? Then why are you coming over here to my house with this BS? How did you know where I live?"

"Don't worry about that. You'd better watch who you're talking to," Frank said.

I guess he thought he was intimidating me, so I told him, "You hold up right here." I went in the house and began changing into my fighting clothes. I was breathing heavily and nervous, but I was shooting stuff off fast. By the time I got down to the bottom of the stairs, Frank was gone. I ran back upstairs and called a few of my friends who didn't mess around. I put them on the three-way line and told them what had happened, what I was going to do, and where I was going to be just in case I needed to get bailed out of jail.

I walked around the corner with a little club in my hand. I walked down Kern Street slowly, wearing all black. I saw Frank talking to someone, and next thing I knew I had struck him with the club, which flew out of my hand. Frank ran a few paces, turned back around with his head down, and rushed me. As I fell to the ground, I pulled his hoodie over his head so he couldn't see.

He struck me twice in the forehead, and I was tagging him back when all of a sudden the friends I had called came out of nowhere and began whooping on Frank. He started running, and we couldn't catch him. I could hear Lucy hollering at us to leave Frank alone. I was shocked to hear her say that because she had told me she had broken up with him and that she would call the cops if he showed up. I thanked Lenny and Richard for showing up the way they did, and we left Kern Street talking about what had happened. I was still breathing heavily and nervous. My adrenaline had kicked into overdrive.

A few days later I got a call from Lucy, and she tried to explain what had happened and why she hadn't called me. I was still upset, but I let her explain. She said she had decided to give Frank another chance because of their son. She didn't want him to grow up without his dad. I understood where she was coming from.

"Why didn't you just call me and tell me?"

"I tried, but every time I picked up the phone he was right there beside me asking me who I was trying to call."

"I know, but who told him where I lived?" I asked.

"I think one of my nosy neighbors, but I'm not sure who. He said he doesn't have any more beef with you, but he wants the other guys who were with you."

I laughed so loud. "Say what? Believe me, he doesn't want any more of them. Well, it was fun while it lasted, Lucy, and I wish you the best of luck."

"I'm so sorry that it had to end like this, Nathan. I really do care for you."

At that point I hung up the phone. I was tired of being hurt by women, and that was why I kept a wall up in relationships. Lucy knew about my past, so how could she let a good thing go like this?

After months of recouping, I was walking to the store when I saw Lucy's friend Camilla. She told me that Lucy missed me. She kept rambling on about how Frank wasn't good for Lucy. I listened to her for a while and then told her, "Please don't tell me any more. Lucy made her choice, and I'm good with that."

Camilla looked at me, startled, and said, "Oh, I'm sorry, Nathan. I just thought you should know."

"Well, thank you for the news anyway."

I looked Camilla up and down several times. Even though she was good looking to me, I just turned my head and started walking home.

See, after going through all these bad relationships, I realized that I couldn't keep trying to get revenge on people because I was only hurting myself. I didn't want to hurt myself anymore. I was getting revenge, but the people who betrayed me didn't even know what I had done behind their backs, so how was it revenge?

I could have slept with Camilla and I could have done more damage to Frank, but the idea of revenge wasn't pleasing my soul like it used to. I realized that I had to put things like that in God's hands. God was the only one who got revenge. I knew one day that he would bring the woman He made for me. I was proud of myself because I had finally become a man.

All these bad relationships and love circles made me realize that in life I was going to lose some battles, but in the end I wouldn't lose the war!

Conclusion

After we sat there and listened to each other's stories, it amazed us how many similarities there were. We had each other's backs in some instances. The great thing about us was that we never turned on each other.

What made us feel good was the fact that we all were men now, and we didn't feel the need to get anybody back anymore. Getting revenge was in our past. As Nathan said, we learned to let God handle things instead.

The jazz house had died down a little, so we took a look around and saw all the single people. This reminded us how blessed we were to have that special someone in our lives. We got up and walked around a little more, admiring the place some more before we decided to go.

"Wow, Lenny, I can't believe you went through all that craziness," Richard said.

"Well, I can't believe you went through all that mess too," I replied.

"Yeah, both of y'all were some low-down nasty men," Nathan said, laughing.

Richard and I tapped Nathan on the back of the head and starting laughing, too.

"Boy, look at the pot calling the kettle black," Richard said to Nathan.

"Guys, guys, I'm just playing. Can't you take a joke?" Nathan said.

We smiled and did a group hug. Then we busted out in laughter. We'd had crazy lives, but we had made it out on top.

We left the jazz house staggering and helped each other to our cars. It was a sight to see. It was a good thing we had parked pretty close to one another.

We decided to go to a breakfast spot. We all met there and continued talking about the past. We all wished we could see what some of the people who did us wrong were doing. I bet their lives were hell.

Then the waitress came over, and we all ordered food. Of course, Nathan and Richard had to start drilling on each other, and they had even the waitress and a lot of other people laughing at their foolishness.

As soon as our food came to our table, so did three beautiful women. We paused for a minute, looked at each other, and said, "Nope." Then we started laughing. I looked at my wedding ring and kissed it.

I had something special and sacred, and the fellas and I knew that. After all our battles, we had won the war, exactly like Nathan had said.

As we finished up the food and got ready to leave, my wife, Nakia, called to ask where I was and what I was doing. I told her, "Nothing, honey. I am on my way, so don't you worry."

"Okay, honey. I was just worried about you. Please make it home safe."

Soon after that, Shant*é* and Jeanette called Nathan and Richard. They looked at me and smiled. We all knew what that meant—we had enjoyed each other just a little too much. Now we had our wives nervous and worried. We hadn't hung out like this in so long, and it felt so good.

We walked out to our cars and chatted a little more. Richard opened his car door and asked, "Isn't it funny how we used to try to get revenge on people who betrayed us, but it seemed as if they never found out about it—or it took so long to get them back? Nowadays if you sit back, God will get those people back so fast."

"Yes, you're right—in the blink of an eye," Nathan said.

"Yeah, the man upstairs doesn't waste any time, so I don't waste my time anymore trying to get anybody back," Lenny said.

"Yeah, too much energy gets wasted."

I guess in life everyone, including my fellas and I, had to learn some valuable lessons. Life was too short, so now we focused on our health and our families. We realized that there were still folks who tried to take things in their own hands like we had. We had found out the hard way that things were out of our hands, and we hoped they would learn too.

I hugged Nathan and Richard and told them we should get together more. It had been a pleasure to spend time with them tonight. We had bonded, and our stories taught us all a lesson. No matter what, we would leave revenge to God because He was the only one who really got revenge in the end.

The End

Review Requested:
If you loved this book, would you please provide a review at Amazon.com?

www.ingramcontent.com/pod-product-compliance
Lightning Source LLC
LaVergne TN
LVHW052055180325
806141LV00008B/241